The Hidden Sanctuary

Rene' Stanley

Rene' Stanley

Cover Design by Rene' Stanley

ISBN: 979-8-9922952-8-3 (paperback)

Library of Congress Control Number: 2024927033

bbr@booksbyrene.com

https://books-by-rene.store

1 edition 2025

Contents

1

Discovery

The sun blazed relentlessly over the vast expanse of the desert, turning the sand into a shimmering sea of gold. Dr. Jonathan Reed, a renowned archaeologist, stood at the edge of an ancient excavation site, his sharp blue eyes scanning the horizon. The heat was oppressive, but it was nothing compared to the fire of curiosity and determination burning within him. He adjusted his wide-brimmed hat, wiping a bead of sweat from his brow, and returned his focus to the dig site.

"Gabriel, over here!" Reed called out, his voice carrying over the hum of activity around the excavation.

Gabriel Martinez, Reed's loyal friend and fellow archaeologist, appeared from behind a crumbling stone wall, his broad smile visible even from a distance. Gabriel was a stocky man with an infectious enthusiasm that often lightened the weight of their arduous work. He approached Reed, his eyes sparkling with excitement.

"Found something, Jonathan?" Gabriel asked, peering at the ground where Reed had been working.

Reed nodded, crouching down to carefully brush away the sand from a partially exposed object. "I think we've hit the jackpot this time. Look at these inscriptions."

Gabriel knelt beside him, examining the faint carvings on the stone. "These markings... they're early Christian symbols. Could this be part of the sanctuary we've been searching for?"

Reed's eyes gleamed behind his wire-rimmed glasses. "It's possible. This might be the breakthrough we've been waiting for."

The manuscript that had led them here was an extraordinary find in itself, discovered in a remote library in Alexandria. It hinted at a hidden sanctuary where early Christians had concealed a powerful relic. The precise nature of the relic was still a mystery, but the manuscript suggested it held immense significance, both historical and spiritual.

"Let's carefully document this and send the images to Emily," Reed suggested. "Her expertise in early Christian history will be invaluable."

Gabriel nodded, pulling out his camera to capture the details. "Emily will be thrilled. She's been waiting for something like this."

As Gabriel worked, Reed stood and gazed across the desert, a sense of unease creeping over him. He couldn't shake the feeling that they were being watched. The vast emptiness of the desert could play tricks on the mind, but Reed had learned to trust his instincts. They had guided him through many perilous situations in his career.

"Jonathan, are you alright?" Gabriel asked, noticing Reed's distant expression.

"Yeah," Reed replied, forcing a smile. "Just the heat getting to me, I guess. Let's wrap up here and head back to camp. We need to start analyzing these findings as soon as possible."

The two men gathered their equipment and made their way back to their temporary camp, a collection of tents and equipment trucks nestled in a shallow valley. The camp was a hive of activity, with their team cataloging artifacts and managing the logistics of the excavation.

As they approached, Reed's satellite phone buzzed. He glanced at the screen and saw Emily Carter's name. Emily was a courageous missionary with a deep passion for early Christian history, and she had been an essential part of their research team, albeit from afar.

"Emily, perfect timing," Reed said, answering the call. "We've found something interesting."

"Jonathan, that's great news!" Emily's voice crackled through the connection. "Send me the details and the images. I'll start analyzing them right away."

"Already on it," Reed replied. "Gabriel is uploading them now. I'll also send you some of the inscriptions we've uncovered. They seem to be in early Christian script."

"Got it," Emily said. "I'll get to work on it immediately. Keep me updated."

Reed ended the call and turned to Gabriel, who was busy transmitting the images and data to Emily. Despite the progress they were making, Reed couldn't shake the feeling that something was amiss. The desert had a way of concealing its secrets, and not all of them were ancient.

As night fell, the temperature dropped sharply, and the camp was illuminated by the soft glow of lanterns. Reed sat at a makeshift desk in his tent, pouring over the images and notes they had taken. Gabriel joined him, his usual jovial demeanor replaced by a more serious expression.

"Jonathan, I've been thinking," Gabriel began, "if this really is the sanctuary, we need to be prepared for anything. The manuscript hinted at dangers beyond just natural hazards."

Reed nodded. "You're right. We've faced our share of challenges, but something about this feels different. More... significant."

Gabriel leaned back in his chair, staring at the tent ceiling. "Do you think Emily will be able to join us here? Her insights could be crucial."

"I hope so," Reed replied. "But we need to be careful. The less attention we draw, the better. We don't know who else might be interested in this discovery."

Their conversation was interrupted by a sudden noise outside the tent. Reed and Gabriel exchanged a glance, both reaching for their flashlights. Stepping outside, they scanned the camp but saw nothing unusual. The desert wind howled softly, rustling the fabric of the tents.

"Probably just the wind," Gabriel said, though his tone lacked conviction.

Reed nodded, but his instincts told him otherwise. They were being watched; of that, he was certain. He just didn't know by whom.

The following morning, the camp was abuzz with the news of their discovery. Reed gathered the team for a briefing, sharing the details of their findings and their next steps.

"We've uncovered inscriptions that suggest we are on the right track," Reed explained. "Our next objective is to locate the sanctuary itself. This will require careful planning and preparation."

One of the team members, a young archaeologist named Laura, raised her hand. "Dr. Reed, what about the security concerns? We've heard rumors about treasure hunters and worse."

Reed nodded. "That's a valid concern. We'll need to increase our security measures and ensure that our findings are kept confidential. Gabriel and I will handle the core excavation work, but we'll need everyone's vigilance."

As the team dispersed to their tasks, Reed felt a sense of purpose and determination. They were on the brink of a significant discovery, one that could shed light on early Christian history in unprecedented ways. But he knew they had to proceed with caution. The desert was unforgiving, and there were always those who would seek to exploit such a discovery for their own gain.

Later that day, Reed and Gabriel returned to the dig site, continuing their meticulous work. The inscriptions they had found were becoming clearer, revealing more details about the sanctuary. As they worked, Reed's thoughts drifted to Emily. He knew she would be invaluable once she joined them on-site.

"Jonathan," Gabriel said, breaking his concentration, "we've got something here."

Reed looked up to see Gabriel holding a fragment of what appeared to be an ancient manuscript. The parchment was fragile, but the writing was legible.

"This matches the style and content of the manuscript we found in Alexandria," Gabriel said excitedly. "It's another piece of the puzzle."

Reed examined the fragment, his mind racing with possibilities. "We're getting closer. This confirms that we're on the right track."

As they documented the new find, Reed couldn't help but feel a mixture of excitement and apprehension. The deeper they delved into this ancient mystery, the more he sensed the presence of unseen forces. The sanctuary was real, and it held secrets that some would kill to possess.

That night, as Reed sat in his tent, he received another call from Emily. She sounded tired but exhilarated.

"Jonathan, I've been going through the inscriptions you sent me," she said. "They are remarkable. I believe they point to a hidden chamber within the sanctuary, one that holds the relic."

Reed's heart pounded. "That's incredible, Emily. Can you join us here? We could use your expertise on-site."

"I'm making arrangements," Emily replied. "I should be there within a few days. In the meantime, be careful. There's a lot more at stake here than just an archaeological find."

"I know," Reed said, his voice steady. "We'll be ready."

As he ended the call, Reed felt a renewed sense of resolve. The path ahead was fraught with danger, but he was determined to uncover the truth. The sanctuary was out there, waiting to reveal its secrets. And with Emily and Gabriel by his side, he was ready to face whatever challenges lay ahead.

The wind howled outside, and the stars shone brightly in the desert sky, bearing silent witness to the unfolding drama. Dr. Jonathan Reed knew that their journey had only just begun, and the true test of their perseverance and faith was yet to come.

2

Introduction to Emily

Emily Carter sat at a large oak table in the center of the historical archives room, surrounded by stacks of ancient texts and manuscripts. The air was filled with the scent of old paper and the quiet hum of the city beyond the library's walls. Her short brown hair was tied back in a practical ponytail, and her piercing brown eyes scanned the pages of a particularly old manuscript with a focused intensity.

This was her sanctuary, a place where the past whispered its secrets to those who were patient enough to listen. Today, she was deep in research, piecing together fragments of early Christian history. Each discovery felt like a small victory, a step closer to understanding the lives and faith of those who came before.

As she meticulously transcribed the faded words, her phone buzzed. She glanced at the screen and saw Dr. Jonathan Reed's name. With a quick swipe, she answered.

"Jonathan, any updates?" Emily asked, her voice tinged with anticipation.

"Emily, we've found something remarkable," Reed's voice crackled through. "An inscription that matches the manuscript from Alexandria. We're piecing together more clues about the sanctuary."

Emily's heart skipped a beat. "That's incredible news! I'll finish up here and head over as soon as I can."

"Great. We need your expertise on-site. This discovery could be monumental," Reed replied.

"I'll be there in a few days. Keep me posted on any developments," Emily said before ending the call.

She took a deep breath, feeling the thrill of impending adventure. This was what she lived for—the chance to uncover history and bring it to light. Gathering her notes, she headed toward the exit, but not before making a stop at the curator's office.

Sophia Grey, the museum curator and a respected historian, looked up from her desk as Emily entered. Her sharp, professional demeanor was softened by a genuine smile.

"Emily, to what do I owe the pleasure?" Sophia asked, removing her glasses and setting them aside.

"I've been working on the early Christian manuscripts," Emily began, "and Jonathan just called. They've made a significant discovery at the dig site. I need to head out there."

Sophia nodded, her interest piqued. "Do you have the details?"

"Not all, but it involves the sanctuary we've been researching. It could be a major breakthrough," Emily explained.

"Then you must go," Sophia said decisively. "This could be a once-in-a-lifetime opportunity. Just promise me you'll be careful."

"I will, Sophia. Thank you for everything," Emily replied, her gratitude evident.

With a nod and a quick embrace, Emily left the library, her mind already racing ahead to the desert and the mysteries it held. She packed her essentials swiftly, including her small cross necklace, a symbol of her faith and a source of comfort.

A few days later, Emily stepped off the small plane that had brought her to the nearest airstrip to the excavation site. The heat hit her like a wall, but she welcomed it, knowing it was part of the journey. She spotted a familiar face in the crowd—Gabriel Martinez, waving enthusiastically.

"Emily! Over here!" Gabriel called out, his broad smile as infectious as ever.

"Gabriel, it's good to see you," Emily said, returning his embrace. "How's Jonathan holding up?"

"As intense as ever," Gabriel replied with a chuckle. "He's been working nonstop since the discovery. Come on, we have a lot to catch up on."

They loaded Emily's bags into a rugged off-road vehicle and set off toward the camp. The desert landscape stretched out before them, a seemingly endless expanse of sand and rock. As they drove, Gabriel filled her in on the latest developments.

"The inscriptions we found match the ones from Alexandria," Gabriel explained. "We're convinced they're pointing us toward the sanctuary, but it's a treacherous path. Natural hazards, potential traps—everything you'd expect from an ancient site meant to protect something valuable."

Emily listened intently, her mind already processing the information. "And the cult? Any signs of them?"

Gabriel's expression darkened. "Not yet, but we're certain they're aware of our progress. We've increased security, but it's a constant concern."

"We'll have to stay vigilant," Emily said. "This discovery is too important to fall into the wrong hands."

They arrived at the camp just as the sun was beginning to set, casting long shadows across the tents and equipment. Reed was waiting for them, his tall figure silhouetted against the twilight. He approached with a warm smile, his deep blue eyes reflecting the light of the setting sun.

"Emily, welcome," Reed said, his voice filled with genuine warmth. "It's good to have you here."

"It's good to be here," Emily replied. "I've been going over the notes Gabriel sent. This is a significant find."

Reed nodded. "Indeed. Let's get you settled in, and then we can discuss our next steps."

Later that evening, they gathered in the main tent, illuminated by lanterns. The atmosphere was a mix of excitement and tension, everyone aware of the gravity of their mission. Reed spread out a series of maps and photographs on the table, pointing to the inscriptions they had found.

"These symbols here," Reed began, "are indicative of early Christian iconography. They're not just random markings; they're a code, a guide to the sanctuary."

Emily leaned in, studying the images. "This matches what we found in Alexandria. If we follow these symbols, they should lead us to the hidden chamber."

"Exactly," Reed agreed. "But the path is fraught with danger. We've already encountered several natural hazards, and we need to be prepared for more."

Gabriel chimed in, his tone serious. "And we can't forget the cult. Anton Graves is ruthless. If he gets wind of our progress, he'll stop at nothing to get to the relic first."

Emily's expression hardened. "Then we need to stay one step ahead. We have to be smart about this."

Reed nodded. "We leave at first light. Get some rest, everyone. Tomorrow, we continue the search."

As the team dispersed, Emily found herself alone with Reed. She could see the strain in his eyes, the weight of responsibility he carried.

"Jonathan, are you alright?" she asked gently.

Reed sighed, running a hand through his sandy brown hair. "I'm fine, Emily. It's just... this discovery, it's more than just an archaeological find. It's personal."

Emily placed a reassuring hand on his arm. "We'll get through this, together. We've faced challenges before, and we've come out stronger."

Reed nodded, a faint smile touching his lips. "Thanks, Emily. Your faith means a lot."

"Faith is what drives us, Jonathan. It's what keeps us going," Emily said softly.

With that, they parted ways, each heading to their tents to rest before the next day's journey. The desert night was cool and still, a stark contrast to the searing heat of the day. Emily lay on her cot, staring up at the canvas ceiling, her mind filled with thoughts of the sanctuary and the relic they sought.

The next morning, the camp was a hive of activity as the team prepared to set out. Emily donned her practical attire, adjusting her cross necklace as a final touch. Reed and Gabriel were already at the dig site, making final preparations.

"Ready for another day of adventure?" Gabriel asked, his tone light but his eyes serious.

"Always," Emily replied with a smile. "Let's find that sanctuary."

They set off into the desert, following the clues from the inscriptions. The landscape was harsh and unforgiving, but they pressed on, driven by a shared sense of purpose. Emily's knowledge of early Christian history proved invaluable as they deciphered more symbols and navigated the treacherous terrain.

As they worked, Reed couldn't help but feel a sense of camaraderie with his team. Despite the dangers and challenges, they were united in their quest. Emily's unwavering faith and Gabriel's resourcefulness were a constant source of strength.

Hours passed as they made their way through the desert, the sun climbing higher in the sky. They reached a particularly challenging section of the path, where the ground was unstable and the risk of landslides was high.

"Careful, everyone," Reed cautioned. "Watch your step."

They moved cautiously, testing each foothold before proceeding. As they navigated the precarious terrain, Emily spotted something unusual—a faint glimmer beneath a layer of sand.

"Jonathan, over here," she called out.

Reed joined her, and together they unearthed a small, ornate box. The craftsmanship was exquisite, and the symbols on the lid matched those they had been following.

"This could be it," Reed said, his voice filled with excitement.

Emily carefully opened the box, revealing a collection of scrolls and a small, intricately carved cross. She gently lifted the cross, examining it closely.

"This is a significant find," she said, her voice reverent. "These scrolls could contain invaluable information about the sanctuary."

Reed nodded, his eyes gleaming with anticipation. "Let's document everything and keep moving. We're getting closer."

They continued their journey, the discovery renewing their determination. As they trekked deeper into the desert, the landscape began to change. The sand gave way to rocky outcrops and ancient ruins, remnants of a civilization long forgotten.

Emily's heart raced as they approached what appeared to be an entrance to a hidden chamber. The inscriptions on the stone walls confirmed it—they had found the sanctuary.

"Everyone, this is it," Reed announced. "We've found the entrance."

The team gathered around, their excitement palpable. Emily's eyes shone with a mixture of awe and determination.

"Let's go in," she said. "We've come this far. We can't stop now."

They carefully made their way into the chamber, the air cool and damp compared to the scorching heat outside. The walls were lined with more inscriptions, telling the story of the early Christians who had sought refuge here.

As they explored the chamber, Emily felt a profound sense of connection to the past. This was more than just a historical site—it was a testament to the resilience and faith of those who had come before.

"Jonathan, look at this," she called out, pointing to a particularly detailed carving. "It's a depiction of the relic."

Reed joined her, studying the carving with fascination. "This confirms it. The relic is here, somewhere within these walls."

As they delved deeper into the chamber, they came across a set of intricate locks and mechanisms, designed to protect the relic from intruders. Gabriel's puzzle-solving skills came into play as he deftly worked to unlock the mechanisms.

"Almost there," Gabriel muttered, his brow furrowed in concentration.

Finally, with a satisfying click, the last lock released. The team held their breath as the door slowly swung open, revealing a small, dimly lit room. In the center of the room, on a stone pedestal, rested the relic—a beautifully crafted cross, glowing faintly in the dim light.

Emily approached the pedestal, her heart pounding. She reached out and gently lifted the relic, feeling a surge of awe and reverence.

"We've found it," she whispered, tears of joy streaming down her face. "We've found the relic."

Reed placed a hand on her shoulder, his own eyes filled with emotion. "We did it, Emily. We found the sanctuary and the relic. This is a monumental achievement."

As they stood there, surrounded by the echoes of the past, they knew that their journey was far from over. The discovery of the relic was just the beginning. The real challenge lay in protecting it from those who sought to exploit its power.

"Let's document everything and get out of here," Reed said, his tone resolute. "We need to ensure the safety of this relic."

Emily nodded, her determination renewed. They had come this far together, and she knew they had the strength and faith to face whatever challenges lay ahead.

As they made their way back to the entrance, the weight of their discovery settled upon them. They had uncovered a piece of history that would change their lives forever, and they were ready to face the trials that awaited them.

The desert sun was setting as they emerged from the chamber, casting long shadows across the ancient ruins. Emily looked back at the entrance, feeling a deep sense of fulfillment and purpose.

"This is just the beginning," she said softly. "There's so much more to discover."

Reed smiled, his eyes reflecting the same determination. "Yes, it is. And we'll face it together."

With that, they began their journey back to the camp, ready to share their incredible discovery with the world and protect the legacy of those who had come before them.

3

Uniting Forces

The morning sun cast a golden hue over the university campus, highlighting the stately buildings and manicured lawns. Dr. Jonathan Reed's study, nestled in the heart of the history department, was a cluttered yet orderly haven of ancient texts, maps, and archaeological tools. The room buzzed with a palpable energy as Reed prepared for the arrival of Emily Carter.

Emily had been a crucial part of their recent discoveries, her knowledge of early Christian history proving invaluable. Today, she was joining Reed and Gabriel Martinez to discuss the next steps in their journey.

Reed glanced at his watch and then at the door. "She should be here any minute," he muttered to himself, shuffling through a stack of notes.

Gabriel, lounging in a chair nearby, grinned. "Relax, Jonathan. Emily's always on time."

As if on cue, there was a knock at the door. Reed opened it to reveal Emily, her face flushed with excitement. She stepped inside, her eyes immediately drawn to the detailed maps spread across Reed's desk.

"Jonathan, Gabriel, it's good to see you both," she greeted, setting her bag down and joining them at the desk.

"Emily, welcome back," Reed said warmly. "We've got a lot to discuss."

"Absolutely," she replied. "I've been reviewing the inscriptions and I think we're on the verge of a major breakthrough."

Gabriel leaned forward, his interest piqued. "What have you found?"

Emily pulled out a notebook and opened it to a page filled with sketches and notes. "These symbols here," she pointed, "they're not just markers. They're part of a map. If we can decode them fully, we'll have the exact location of the hidden chamber."

Reed's eyes lit up. "That's fantastic, Emily. Let's get to work."

They spent the next few hours poring over the inscriptions and comparing them to the maps and texts they had collected. The atmosphere was one of intense concentration, broken only by the occasional exchange of ideas and insights.

"Look at this," Emily said, pointing to a particular symbol. "This matches a location we identified earlier, but we missed the connection. It's a marker for an ancient route used by early Christians."

Gabriel nodded, his eyes scanning the page. "If we follow this route, it should lead us directly to the sanctuary."

Reed tapped his pen against the desk, deep in thought. "We'll need to be careful. The cult is likely aware of our progress. We can't afford any missteps."

Emily agreed. "We need to stay one step ahead. This discovery is too important to fall into the wrong hands."

As they continued their work, Reed felt a growing sense of urgency. They were on the cusp of something monumental, but the dangers were real. The cult, led by the ruthless Anton Graves, would stop at nothing to obtain the relic.

"Emily, Gabriel," Reed said, breaking the silence, "we need to plan our next move carefully. Let's regroup this evening and finalize our strategy."

Later that evening, the team gathered in Reed's study once more, the room bathed in the soft glow of lamplight. The maps and notes were spread out before them, a testament to their relentless pursuit of knowledge.

"We're close," Reed began, his voice steady. "But we need to be strategic. We can't let Graves and his followers get the upper hand."

Gabriel leaned back in his chair, his expression serious. "We should expect resistance. Graves has resources and he's not afraid to use them."

Emily nodded, her face determined. "We need to move quickly and quietly. The less attention we draw, the better."

Reed agreed. "We'll leave at first light. Emily, you'll take point on navigating the route. Gabriel, you and I will handle the logistics and security."

Gabriel grinned. "Sounds like a plan. Let's get some rest and be ready for tomorrow."

As they prepared to leave, Emily pulled Reed aside. "Jonathan, are you sure you're ready for this? You've been pushing yourself hard."

Reed gave her a reassuring smile. "I'm fine, Emily. This is too important to hesitate now. We'll make it through, together."

She nodded, her concern evident. "Alright. Just promise me you'll take care of yourself."

"I promise," Reed replied.

With that, they parted ways, each heading to their quarters to rest before the journey ahead. The night was quiet, the campus cloaked in darkness, but the sense of anticipation was almost tangible.

The next morning, the team assembled at the edge of the campus, their gear packed and ready. The sun had just begun to rise, casting a warm glow over the landscape.

"Everyone ready?" Reed asked, his voice filled with determination.

"Ready," Emily and Gabriel replied in unison.

They set off, following the ancient route that Emily had decoded. The path led them through dense forests and rugged terrain, each step bringing them closer to their goal.

As they walked, they kept a vigilant eye on their surroundings, aware of the potential dangers. The cult had eyes everywhere, and they couldn't afford to be caught off guard.

After several hours of trekking, they reached a clearing that matched the location marked on the map. Reed signaled for them to stop, his eyes scanning the area.

"This is it," he said quietly. "The entrance to the hidden chamber should be nearby."

Emily studied the map and the inscriptions, her brow furrowed in concentration. "There," she pointed to a rocky outcrop. "The entrance is hidden behind those rocks."

Gabriel moved forward, inspecting the rocks. "There's a mechanism here. It's well-hidden, but I can unlock it."

Reed and Emily watched as Gabriel carefully manipulated the mechanism. With a soft click, the rocks shifted, revealing a narrow passageway.

"Nice work, Gabriel," Reed said, clapping him on the shoulder.

Gabriel grinned. "Just like old times, huh?"

They entered the passageway, the air cool and damp compared to the outside. The walls were lined with more inscriptions, telling the story of the early Christians who had sought refuge here.

"This is incredible," Emily whispered, her voice filled with awe. "We're walking through history."

Reed nodded, his eyes wide with wonder. "Let's document everything carefully. This is a significant find."

As they made their way deeper into the chamber, they encountered a series of intricate locks and traps designed to protect the relic. Gabriel's puzzle-solving skills once again proved invaluable as he deftly navigated the obstacles.

"Almost there," Gabriel muttered, his brow furrowed in concentration.

Finally, they reached a large, ornate door. The symbols on the door matched those they had been following, confirming that they had found the hidden chamber.

"Everyone ready?" Reed asked, his voice steady despite the tension in the air.

"Ready," Emily and Gabriel replied.

Reed carefully opened the door, revealing a small, dimly lit room. In the center of the room, on a stone pedestal, rested the relic—a beautifully crafted cross, glowing faintly in the dim light.

Emily approached the pedestal, her heart pounding. She reached out and gently lifted the relic, feeling a surge of awe and reverence.

"We've found it," she whispered, tears of joy streaming down her face. "We've found the relic."

Reed placed a hand on her shoulder, his own eyes filled with emotion. "We did it, Emily. We found the sanctuary and the relic. This is a monumental achievement."

As they stood there, surrounded by the echoes of the past, they knew that their journey was far from over. The discovery of the relic was just the beginning. The real challenge lay in protecting it from those who sought to exploit its power.

"Let's document everything and get out of here," Reed said, his tone resolute. "We need to ensure the safety of this relic."

Emily nodded, her determination renewed. They had come this far together, and she knew they had the strength and faith to face whatever challenges lay ahead.

As they made their way back to the entrance, the weight of their discovery settled upon them. They had uncovered a piece of history that would change their lives forever, and they were ready to face the trials that awaited them.

The desert sun was setting as they emerged from the chamber, casting long shadows across the ancient ruins. Emily looked back at the entrance, feeling a deep sense of fulfillment and purpose.

"This is just the beginning," she said softly. "There's so much more to discover."

Reed smiled, his eyes reflecting the same determination. "Yes, it is. And we'll face it together."

With that, they began their journey back to the camp, ready to share their incredible discovery with the world and protect the legacy of those who had come before them.

Later that night, as they sat around the campfire, the team reflected on their journey and the challenges ahead. The flickering flames cast a warm glow over their faces, creating a sense of camaraderie and shared purpose.

"Today was a big step forward," Gabriel said, breaking the silence. "But we need to stay vigilant. Graves won't give up easily."

Emily nodded, her expression serious. "We've got the relic, but the real battle is just beginning. We need to be prepared for anything."

Reed looked around at his team, feeling a deep sense of pride and gratitude. "We've come a long way, and we've done it together. No matter what happens, we'll face it as a team."

Gabriel raised his canteen in a toast. "To the hidden sanctuary, and to the journey ahead."

"To the journey ahead," Emily and Reed echoed, clinking their canteens together.

As the night wore on, they shared stories and laughter, the bond between them growing stronger with each passing moment. They knew that the road ahead would be fraught with danger, but they were ready to face it, united by their shared mission and their unwavering faith.

The next morning, they rose with the sun, ready to continue their journey. Emily and Gabriel packed up their gear while Reed reviewed their notes and maps, ensuring they had everything they needed.

"Ready to go?" Reed asked, looking up from his notes.

"Ready," Emily and Gabriel replied.

They set off once more, following the ancient route that would lead them to the next phase of their journey. The landscape was harsh and unforgiving, but they pressed on, driven by a shared sense of purpose.

As they walked, they kept a vigilant eye on their surroundings, aware of the potential dangers. The cult had eyes everywhere, and they couldn't afford to be caught off guard.

After several hours of trekking, they reached a clearing that matched the location marked on the map. Reed signaled for them to stop, his eyes scanning the area.

"This is it," he said quietly. "The entrance to the hidden chamber should be nearby."

Emily studied the map and the inscriptions, her brow furrowed in concentration. "There," she pointed to a rocky outcrop. "The entrance is hidden behind those rocks."

Gabriel moved forward, inspecting the rocks. "There's a mechanism here. It's well-hidden, but I can unlock it."

Reed and Emily watched as Gabriel carefully manipulated the mechanism. With a soft click, the rocks shifted, revealing a narrow passageway.

"Nice work, Gabriel," Reed said, clapping him on the shoulder.

Gabriel grinned. "Just like old times, huh?"

They entered the passageway, the air cool and damp compared to the outside. The walls were lined with more inscriptions, telling the story of the early Christians who had sought refuge here.

"This is incredible," Emily whispered, her voice filled with awe. "We're walking through history."

Reed nodded, his eyes wide with wonder. "Let's document everything carefully. This is a significant find."

As they made their way deeper into the chamber, they encountered a series of intricate locks and traps designed to protect the relic. Gabriel's puzzle-solving skills once again proved invaluable as he deftly navigated the obstacles.

"Almost there," Gabriel muttered, his brow furrowed in concentration.

Finally, they reached a large, ornate door. The symbols on the door matched those they had been following, confirming that they had found the hidden chamber.

"Everyone ready?" Reed asked, his voice steady despite the tension in the air.

"Ready," Emily and Gabriel replied.

Reed carefully opened the door, revealing a small, dimly lit room. In the center of the room, on a stone pedestal, rested the relic—a beautifully crafted cross, glowing faintly in the dim light.

Emily approached the pedestal, her heart pounding. She reached out and gently lifted the relic, feeling a surge of awe and reverence.

"We've found it," she whispered, tears of joy streaming down her face. "We've found the relic."

Reed placed a hand on her shoulder, his own eyes filled with emotion. "We did it, Emily. We found the sanctuary and the relic. This is a monumental achievement."

As they stood there, surrounded by the echoes of the past, they knew that their journey was far from over. The discovery of the relic was just the beginning. The real challenge lay in protecting it from those who sought to exploit its power.

"Let's document everything and get out of here," Reed said, his tone resolute. "We need to ensure the safety of this relic."

Emily nodded, her determination renewed. They had come this far together, and she knew they had the strength and faith to face whatever challenges lay ahead.

As they made their way back to the entrance, the weight of their discovery settled upon them. They had uncovered a piece of history that would change their lives forever, and they were ready to face the trials that awaited them.

The desert sun was setting as they emerged from the chamber, casting long shadows across the ancient ruins. Emily looked back at the entrance, feeling a deep sense of fulfillment and purpose.

"This is just the beginning," she said softly. "There's so much more to discover."

Reed smiled, his eyes reflecting the same determination. "Yes, it is. And we'll face it together."

With that, they began their journey back to the camp, ready to share their incredible discovery with the world and protect the legacy of those who had come before them.

4

The First Clue

The sun was just beginning to rise, casting long shadows over the desert as Dr. Jonathan Reed, Emily Carter, and Gabriel Martinez stood at the edge of the ancient ruins. The air was still cool, a brief respite before the day's heat set in. They had spent the previous night discussing their plans and were now ready to follow the clues that would hopefully lead them to the hidden sanctuary.

"Alright, everyone," Reed said, adjusting his hat against the sun's early rays. "We've got a long day ahead. Emily, you have the map and the decoded symbols. Gabriel, you're on logistics and security. Let's move out."

Emily nodded, pulling out the carefully preserved map from her backpack. "The first marker should be about half a mile east of here. We'll need to navigate through this rocky terrain."

Gabriel gave a mock salute. "Ready and able. Let's find ourselves a sanctuary."

They set off, the crunch of their boots against the rocky ground the only sound in the still morning. The terrain was challenging, with uneven paths and jagged rocks that required careful navigation. But they moved with purpose, driven by the significance of their mission.

After about an hour of trekking, Emily halted abruptly. "Hold up," she called out, kneeling to inspect a large boulder. "I think this is it."

Reed and Gabriel joined her, peering at the faint inscriptions on the rock. Reed's eyes lit up as he recognized the symbols. "This is definitely one of the markers. Good find, Emily."

Emily traced the carvings with her fingers. "It's a warning. It mentions natural hazards ahead. We'll need to be cautious."

Gabriel scanned the area, his eyes narrowing. "Hazards are one thing, but we also need to keep an eye out for Graves and his followers. This place is too important to be left unguarded."

Reed nodded. "Agreed. We proceed with caution. Emily, lead the way."

As they continued, the terrain became increasingly difficult. The path narrowed, flanked by steep cliffs on one side and a drop into a ravine on the other. They moved slowly, each step deliberate and measured.

"Watch your step," Gabriel warned, helping Emily over a particularly tricky section. "One wrong move and it's a long way down."

Emily smiled gratefully. "Thanks, Gabriel. I appreciate it."

Reed, a few steps ahead, called back to them. "There's another marker up here. We're on the right track."

They gathered around the new marker, examining the symbols. Emily translated them quickly. "It's a direction. We need to head north from here."

Gabriel sighed, glancing up at the sky. "North it is. Let's keep moving."

The sun climbed higher, and the heat became oppressive. They took frequent breaks, drinking water and resting in the shade whenever they could find it. Despite the challenging conditions, their spirits remained high.

"This is what it's all about," Gabriel said during one of their breaks. "The adventure, the discovery. There's nothing like it."

Emily nodded, wiping sweat from her brow. "It's exhausting, but worth every moment. We're uncovering history here."

Reed smiled, his eyes fixed on the horizon. "And we're doing it together. That's what makes it all worthwhile."

As they continued, the landscape began to change. The rocky terrain gave way to a series of dunes, the sand shifting beneath their feet. Emily consulted the map frequently, ensuring they stayed on the correct path.

"We're getting closer," she said, her voice filled with excitement. "The next marker should be just ahead."

They crested a dune and found themselves overlooking a vast expanse of desert. In the distance, they could see the outline of ancient ruins, partially buried in the sand.

"There it is," Reed said, a sense of awe in his voice. "The next clue."

They descended the dune carefully, making their way toward the ruins. As they approached, the scale of the site became apparent. Massive stone structures, worn by time and the elements, stood as silent sentinels over the desert.

"This is incredible," Emily whispered. "These ruins are ancient, predating most known civilizations."

Gabriel whistled softly. "Imagine what secrets they hold."

Reed led the way into the ruins, his eyes scanning for any signs of the next marker. They moved cautiously, aware that they could be watched.

"Stay alert," Reed warned. "Graves could have left traps or be lying in wait."

They searched the ruins meticulously, examining every stone and inscription. Finally, Emily found what they were looking for—a series of symbols carved into a hidden alcove.

"Here it is," she called out. "This is the next clue."

Reed and Gabriel joined her, studying the symbols. Reed's eyes narrowed in concentration. "It's a riddle. Something about the light revealing the path."

Gabriel frowned. "The light? What does that mean?"

Emily thought for a moment. "It could be referring to the sun. We need to wait for the right time of day when the light hits these ruins in a specific way."

Reed nodded. "That makes sense. Let's set up camp and observe the ruins as the sun moves. We'll document everything and be ready to move when the light reveals the path."

They set up a temporary camp within the shelter of the ruins, using the time to rest and prepare. As the day wore on, they took turns watching the shadows and light play across the ancient stones.

Late in the afternoon, as the sun began to dip toward the horizon, Emily noticed a change. "Look, over there," she pointed. "The light is hitting that wall differently."

Reed and Gabriel turned to see the sunlight illuminating a previously hidden passage. "That's it," Reed said, his voice filled with excitement. "The light reveals the path."

They quickly packed up their gear and made their way toward the illuminated wall. The passage was narrow and dark, but they entered with determination, their flashlights cutting through the gloom.

The air inside was cool and damp, a stark contrast to the heat outside. The walls were covered in more inscriptions, telling the story of the early Christians who had used this sanctuary.

"This is it," Emily said, her voice echoing in the passage. "We're walking through history."

Reed nodded, his eyes wide with wonder. "Let's keep moving. There's more to discover."

They followed the passage deeper into the ruins, the sense of anticipation growing with each step. As they turned a corner, they came upon a large chamber, its walls adorned with intricate carvings and symbols.

"This is amazing," Gabriel said, his voice filled with awe. "We've found the heart of the sanctuary."

Emily's eyes were drawn to a central pedestal, upon which rested a small, intricately carved box. She approached it carefully, her hands trembling with excitement.

"This could be it," she whispered. "The next clue."

Reed and Gabriel joined her, their eyes fixed on the box. "Open it," Reed said softly. "Let's see what we've found."

Emily carefully lifted the lid, revealing a collection of ancient scrolls and a small, ornate key. "This is incredible," she said, her voice filled with emotion. "These scrolls could contain invaluable information about the sanctuary."

Gabriel examined the key. "And this key... it must unlock something important."

Reed nodded. "Let's document everything and figure out our next move. We're getting closer."

As they worked, the sense of accomplishment and anticipation was palpable. They were uncovering pieces of history that had been hidden for centuries, and each discovery brought them closer to the ultimate goal—the hidden sanctuary and the relic it contained.

But as they packed up to leave, Reed couldn't shake a sense of unease. The cult had been suspiciously quiet, and he knew they couldn't let their guard down.

"Stay sharp," he warned. "We've made progress, but the danger is far from over. Graves won't give up easily."

Emily and Gabriel nodded, their expressions serious. They knew the stakes were high, and they were ready to face whatever challenges lay ahead.

That evening, back at their camp, they gathered around the fire, discussing their findings and planning their next steps. The night was cool and clear, the stars twinkling overhead.

"These scrolls are incredible," Emily said, carefully unrolling one of them. "They detail the construction of the sanctuary and the precautions taken to protect it."

Gabriel looked at the ornate key. "And this key... it must unlock something significant. We just need to figure out what."

Reed nodded, deep in thought. "The inscriptions mentioned a hidden chamber. This key could be the way to access it. We need to cross-reference the scrolls with the map and the clues we've found so far."

Emily agreed. "We're getting closer. The next step is to decipher these scrolls and determine the exact location of the hidden chamber."

Gabriel grinned. "I love a good puzzle. Let's get to work."

They spent the next few hours meticulously examining the scrolls, comparing them to the map and the inscriptions they had documented. The firelight flickered as they worked, casting long shadows over their faces.

"This passage here," Emily said, pointing to a section of one of the scrolls. "It mentions a hidden mechanism within the central chamber. That must be where the key fits."

Reed's eyes lit up. "That makes sense. If we can find and activate the mechanism, it should reveal the hidden chamber."

Gabriel nodded, his excitement evident. "We're on the right track. Let's get some rest and be ready to explore the central chamber at first light."

As they settled down for the night, Reed couldn't help but feel a sense of pride and anticipation. They had come so far and uncovered so much, but the real challenge was still ahead. The hidden sanctuary and its relic were within reach, but they had to be careful. The cult was still out there, and Graves was a formidable opponent.

"Stay vigilant," Reed reminded them as they drifted off to sleep. "We've made progress, but the real test is yet to come."

The next morning, they rose with the sun, their determination renewed. They packed up their gear and made their way back to the central chamber, ready to unlock its secrets.

The chamber was just as they had left it, the ornate box still resting on the pedestal. Emily took out the key and approached a section of the wall that the scrolls had indicated.

"Here goes nothing," she said, inserting the key into a hidden slot.

There was a soft click, and the wall began to shift, revealing a hidden passage. Reed, Emily, and Gabriel exchanged triumphant looks.

"We did it," Reed said, his voice filled with excitement. "Let's see what's inside."

They entered the hidden passage, their flashlights illuminating the way. The air was cool and musty, the walls lined with more intricate carvings. As they moved deeper, the passage opened up into a large, domed chamber.

In the center of the chamber stood a stone altar, upon which rested a beautifully crafted cross, glowing faintly in the dim light. Emily approached the altar, her heart pounding with excitement.

"This is it," she whispered. "The relic."

Reed and Gabriel joined her, their eyes wide with awe. "We've found it," Reed said softly. "This is a monumental achievement."

As they stood there, surrounded by the echoes of the past, they knew that their journey was far from over. The discovery of the relic was just the beginning. The real challenge lay in protecting it from those who sought to exploit its power.

"Let's document everything and get out of here," Reed said, his tone resolute. "We need to ensure the safety of this relic."

Emily nodded, her determination renewed. They had come this far together, and she knew they had the strength and faith to face whatever challenges lay ahead.

As they made their way back to the entrance, the weight of their discovery settled upon them. They had uncovered a piece of history that would change their lives forever, and they were ready to face the trials that awaited them.

The desert sun was setting as they emerged from the chamber, casting long shadows across the ancient ruins. Emily looked back at the entrance, feeling a deep sense of fulfillment and purpose.

"This is just the beginning," she said softly. "There's so much more to discover."

Reed smiled, his eyes reflecting the same determination. "Yes, it is. And we'll face it together."

With that, they began their journey back to the camp, ready to share their incredible discovery with the world and protect the legacy of those who had come before them.

5

The Cult's Shadow

The sun hung high in the sky, casting harsh shadows over the camp as Dr. Jonathan Reed, Emily Carter, and Gabriel Martinez gathered around a table cluttered with maps, notebooks, and ancient scrolls. The discovery of the relic had injected a new sense of urgency into their mission. They knew the danger that lurked just beyond their sight—the cult led by Anton Graves was never far behind.

"We need to move quickly," Reed said, his tone urgent. "Now that we have the relic, Graves will stop at nothing to take it from us."

Emily nodded, her expression serious. "Agreed. We need to figure out our next steps. The relic is important, but we also need to understand its significance. These scrolls might have more information."

Gabriel leaned back in his chair, arms crossed. "I'll handle the logistics. We need to fortify the camp and ensure we're ready for any potential attacks."

"Good idea," Reed said. "We can't afford to be caught off guard."

As they discussed their plans, the tension in the air was palpable. The threat of Graves and his followers was a constant shadow over their work, a reminder of the high stakes involved in their quest.

Meanwhile, in a dimly lit room in a nearby city, Anton Graves sat at a large wooden table, his sharp features illuminated by the flickering candlelight. He leaned forward, eyes cold and calculating as he spoke to his second-in-command, Marcus Kane.

"They've found the relic," Graves said, his voice low and menacing. "We need to act swiftly. The longer they have it, the harder it will be to take it from them."

Kane, a hulking figure with a menacing presence, nodded. "I'll assemble the team. We'll move in under the cover of darkness and take what's ours."

Graves smiled, a chilling expression that sent a shiver down Kane's spine. "Good. Make sure you don't fail. The relic holds power beyond comprehension, and it belongs to us."

Back at the camp, the team worked tirelessly, analyzing the scrolls and preparing for any potential threats. Emily and Reed were hunched over a particularly detailed scroll, their heads close together as they deciphered the ancient text.

"This part here," Emily said, pointing to a section of the scroll, "mentions a hidden chamber beneath the main sanctuary. It's protected by a series of traps and only accessible through a specific sequence of actions."

Reed's eyes narrowed in concentration. "If we can find that chamber, it might provide us with more context about the relic. But we need to be careful. Graves will likely know about this as well."

Gabriel entered the tent, his face grim. "We've reinforced the perimeter and set up additional security measures. But we need to be prepared for an attack. Graves won't hesitate to use force."

Reed nodded. "We'll take turns keeping watch tonight. We can't afford to let our guard down."

As night fell, the camp was bathed in the soft glow of lanterns. The team gathered around the fire, discussing their plans and sharing a meal. Despite the looming threat, there was a sense of camaraderie and determination among them.

"Emily, what do you think the significance of the relic is?" Gabriel asked, his tone curious.

Emily took a deep breath, her gaze thoughtful. "The relic is more than just a historical artifact. It's a symbol of faith and resilience. The early Christians who hid it believed it held the power to protect and guide them. If Graves gets his hands on it, he could use it for unimaginable harm."

Reed nodded in agreement. "That's why we need to protect it at all costs. This isn't just about history; it's about the future."

Gabriel's expression hardened. "We'll do whatever it takes. Graves won't get his hands on it. Not while we're here."

As the fire crackled and the night deepened, they took turns keeping watch, eyes scanning the darkness for any sign of danger. The quiet of the desert was both a comfort and a source of unease, the silence heavy with anticipation.

In the early hours of the morning, just as the first light began to touch the horizon, Emily, who was on watch, noticed movement at the edge of the camp. She squinted into the darkness, trying to make out the figures moving stealthily toward them.

"Jonathan, Gabriel," she whispered urgently, shaking them awake. "We've got company."

Reed and Gabriel were on their feet in an instant, grabbing their gear and preparing for the worst. The camp erupted into controlled chaos as everyone took their positions, ready to defend themselves.

Graves' followers moved swiftly, their dark forms blending into the shadows as they approached the camp. Marcus Kane led the charge, his eyes fixed on the tent where the relic was kept.

"Spread out," Reed ordered, his voice calm but firm. "Don't let them get to the relic."

The clash was sudden and fierce. Graves' followers were well-trained and ruthless, but the team was prepared. They fought with determination, driven by the knowledge of what was at stake.

Gabriel took on two attackers at once, his movements swift and precise. "Emily, watch your back!" he shouted, deflecting a blow aimed at her.

Emily spun around, her heart pounding as she faced another attacker. She fought with a fierce determination, her mind focused on protecting the relic.

Reed moved through the chaos with practiced ease, his eyes constantly scanning for threats. He spotted Marcus Kane making his way toward the tent and intercepted him, their eyes locking in a moment of recognition.

"Graves sent you, didn't he?" Reed said, his voice cold.

Kane sneered. "You're not getting out of this alive, Reed. The relic belongs to us."

Reed's expression hardened. "Over my dead body."

They clashed, the sounds of their struggle echoing through the camp. Despite Kane's strength and ruthlessness, Reed held his ground, his determination unwavering.

Meanwhile, Emily and Gabriel fought side by side, their movements synchronized as they defended the camp. The battle was intense, but they refused to give in.

"We're not letting them take it," Emily said, her voice filled with resolve.

Gabriel nodded. "We'll hold the line."

As the fight continued, the first light of dawn began to break, casting a faint glow over the camp. The attackers, realizing they were outmatched, began to retreat, pulling back into the shadows.

"Don't let them escape," Reed called out, but it was too late. The remaining attackers had melted into the darkness, leaving behind a scene of chaos and destruction.

The team regrouped, assessing the damage and tending to their wounds. Despite the intensity of the battle, they had managed to protect the relic and drive off Graves' followers.

"Is everyone alright?" Reed asked, his eyes scanning the group.

"We're fine," Emily replied, her voice steady despite the adrenaline still coursing through her veins. "They didn't get the relic."

Gabriel wiped the sweat from his brow, a relieved smile on his face. "We held them off. But they'll be back."

Reed nodded. "We need to stay vigilant. This was just the beginning."

As they cleaned up the camp and prepared for the next stage of their journey, the reality of their situation settled in. The fight to protect the relic was far from over, and the danger was ever-present.

Later that morning, as the team gathered to discuss their next steps, Reed addressed them with a determined expression. "We need to move quickly. The hidden chamber beneath the sanctuary is our next objective. It might provide us with more information about the relic and how to protect it."

Emily nodded, her eyes filled with determination. "Agreed. We can't afford to stay here any longer. Graves knows our location, and he won't stop until he has the relic."

Gabriel packed up his gear, his movements efficient and focused. "Let's get moving. The sooner we find that chamber, the better."

As they set off once more, the desert landscape stretched out before them, a stark reminder of the challenges they faced. The path was difficult, but their resolve was unwavering. They knew what was at stake, and they were prepared to face whatever dangers lay ahead.

The journey to the hidden chamber was fraught with obstacles, the desert terrain proving to be as challenging as ever. But they pressed on, driven by their shared mission and the knowledge that time was against them.

After several hours of trekking, they reached the location indicated by the scrolls. A series of ancient steps led down into the earth, the entrance hidden by centuries of sand and rock.

"This is it," Emily said, her voice filled with excitement and trepidation. "The entrance to the hidden chamber."

Reed nodded, his eyes scanning the area for any signs of danger. "Let's be cautious. We don't know what's down there."

Gabriel took the lead, carefully descending the steps and checking for traps. "Looks clear so far," he called back. "But stay alert."

They followed him down into the darkness, their flashlights cutting through the gloom. The air grew cooler as they descended, the walls lined with intricate carvings and symbols.

"This place is incredible," Emily whispered, her voice echoing in the chamber. "The history here... it's overwhelming."

Reed nodded, his eyes wide with awe. "We're walking through centuries of history. Let's document everything carefully."

As they moved deeper into the chamber, they encountered a series of puzzles and mechanisms designed to protect the relic. Gabriel's puzzle-solving skills once again proved invaluable as he deftly navigated the obstacles.

"Almost there," Gabriel muttered, his brow furrowed in concentration. "Just one more lock."

With a satisfying click, the final lock released, revealing a hidden room. The team entered cautiously, their eyes widening at the sight before them.

The room was filled with ancient artifacts and scrolls, each one a testament to the faith and resilience of the early Christians who had hidden them here. In the center of the room stood a stone altar, upon which rested another beautifully crafted cross, glowing faintly in the dim light.

"This is incredible," Emily said, her voice filled with awe. "We've found another part of the sanctuary."

Reed approached the altar, his eyes fixed on the cross. "This is a significant find. It could provide us with more information about the relic."

As they carefully documented their discovery, the sense of accomplishment and anticipation was palpable. They were uncovering pieces of history that had been hidden for centuries, and each discovery brought them closer to understanding the true significance of the relic.

But as they prepared to leave, Reed couldn't shake a sense of unease. The cult had been suspiciously quiet, and he knew they couldn't let their guard down.

"Stay sharp," he warned. "We've made progress, but the danger is far from over. Graves won't give up easily."

Emily and Gabriel nodded, their expressions serious. They knew the stakes were high, and they were ready to face whatever challenges lay ahead.

That evening, back at their camp, they gathered around the fire, discussing their findings and planning their next steps. The night was cool and clear, the stars twinkling overhead.

"These scrolls are incredible," Emily said, carefully unrolling one of them. "They detail the construction of the sanctuary and the precautions taken to protect it."

Gabriel looked at the ornate cross. "And this cross... it must hold some significance. We need to figure out what it means."

Reed nodded, deep in thought. "The inscriptions mentioned a hidden mechanism within the central chamber. This cross could be the key to accessing it. We need to cross-reference the scrolls with the map and the clues we've found so far."

Emily agreed. "We're getting closer. The next step is to decipher these scrolls and determine the exact location of the hidden chamber."

Gabriel grinned. "I love a good puzzle. Let's get to work."

They spent the next few hours meticulously examining the scrolls, comparing them to the map and the inscriptions they had documented. The firelight flickered as they worked, casting long shadows over their faces.

"This passage here," Emily said, pointing to a section of one of the scrolls. "It mentions a hidden mechanism within the central chamber. That must be where the cross fits."

Reed's eyes lit up. "That makes sense. If we can find and activate the mechanism, it should reveal the hidden chamber."

Gabriel nodded, his excitement evident. "We're on the right track. Let's get some rest and be ready to explore the central chamber at first light."

As they settled down for the night, Reed couldn't help but feel a sense of pride and anticipation. They had come so far and uncovered so much, but the real challenge was still ahead. The hidden sanctuary and its relic were within reach, but they had to be careful. The cult was still out there, and Graves was a formidable opponent.

"Stay vigilant," Reed reminded them as they drifted off to sleep. "We've made progress, but the real test is yet to come."

The next morning, they rose with the sun, their determination renewed. They packed up their gear and made their way back to the central chamber, ready to unlock its secrets.

The chamber was just as they had left it, the ornate cross still resting on the altar. Emily took out the cross and approached a section of the wall that the scrolls had indicated.

"Here goes nothing," she said, inserting the cross into a hidden slot.

There was a soft click, and the wall began to shift, revealing a hidden passage. Reed, Emily, and Gabriel exchanged triumphant looks.

"We did it," Reed said, his voice filled with excitement. "Let's see what's inside."

They entered the hidden passage, their flashlights illuminating the way. The air was cool and musty, the walls lined with more intricate carvings. As they moved deeper, the passage opened up into a large, domed chamber.

In the center of the chamber stood a stone altar, upon which rested a beautifully crafted cross, glowing faintly in the dim light. Emily approached the altar, her heart pounding with excitement.

"This is it," she whispered. "The relic."

Reed and Gabriel joined her, their eyes wide with awe. "We've found it," Reed said softly. "This is a monumental achievement."

As they stood there, surrounded by the echoes of the past, they knew that their journey was far from over. The discovery of the relic was just the beginning. The real challenge lay in protecting it from those who sought to exploit its power.

"Let's document everything and get out of here," Reed said, his tone resolute. "We need to ensure the safety of this relic."

Emily nodded, her determination renewed. They had come this far together, and she knew they had the strength and faith to face whatever challenges lay ahead.

As they made their way back to the entrance, the weight of their discovery settled upon them. They had uncovered a piece of history that would change their lives forever, and they were ready to face the trials that awaited them.

The desert sun was setting as they emerged from the chamber, casting long shadows across the ancient ruins. Emily looked back at the entrance, feeling a deep sense of fulfillment and purpose.

"This is just the beginning," she said softly. "There's so much more to discover."

Reed smiled, his eyes reflecting the same determination. "Yes, it is. And we'll face it together."

With that, they began their journey back to the camp, ready to share their incredible discovery with the world and protect the legacy of those who had come before them.

6

Pastor Miguel's Guidance

The sun was high and unrelenting as Dr. Jonathan Reed, Emily Carter, and Gabriel Martinez trudged back to their camp, the weight of their recent discoveries pressing heavily on their minds. The relic was secure for now, but they all knew that their journey was far from over. They needed answers, and they needed them quickly.

"We can't keep staying here," Reed said, breaking the silence as they approached the tents. "Graves will be back with more force next time."

Emily nodded, wiping sweat from her brow. "Agreed. We need to find a safer location, and we need guidance. The scrolls mentioned someone who could help us—Father Miguel."

Gabriel looked up, his curiosity piqued. "Father Miguel? The same one we read about in the manuscripts?"

"Yes," Emily replied. "He's a wise and enigmatic priest who has deep knowledge of early Christian history. If anyone can help us understand the relic and the sanctuary, it's him."

Reed nodded thoughtfully. "Then we need to find him. Do we know where he is?"

Emily pulled out a map, pointing to a remote monastery nestled in the mountains. "According to the manuscripts, he resides here. It's a long journey, but it's our best shot."

"Then we should pack up and leave as soon as possible," Gabriel said, already moving toward his tent. "No time to waste."

The journey to the monastery was arduous. The desert heat gave way to rugged mountain terrain, each step taking them higher into the cool, crisp air. Despite the physical challenge, their spirits remained high, driven by the hope that Father Miguel would provide the answers they so desperately needed.

"How much farther?" Gabriel asked, his breath coming in short bursts as they climbed.

"Not far now," Emily replied, consulting the map. "We should reach the monastery by late afternoon."

As they continued their ascent, the outline of the monastery began to appear against the rocky backdrop. It was an ancient structure, weathered by time but still standing strong, a testament to its historical significance.

"There it is," Reed said, pointing ahead. "Let's hope Father Miguel is as wise as the manuscripts suggest."

When they finally reached the entrance, they were greeted by a serene silence. The massive wooden doors creaked open, revealing a courtyard filled with the scent of blooming flowers and the soft murmur of prayer.

A monk approached, his eyes filled with a calm wisdom. "Welcome, travelers. How may we assist you?"

"We're here to see Father Miguel," Reed said. "We've come a long way and urgently need his guidance."

The monk nodded. "Follow me. Father Miguel is expecting you."

They followed him through the courtyard and into a dimly lit hall, where they found Father Miguel seated at a simple wooden table, surrounded by ancient texts. He looked up as they entered, his eyes reflecting a deep and peaceful wisdom.

"Welcome," Father Miguel said, his voice gentle but strong. "I have been expecting you."

Reed stepped forward, bowing slightly in respect. "Father Miguel, we need your help. We've found a relic of great significance, and we believe you can help us understand its true purpose."

Father Miguel nodded, gesturing for them to sit. "Tell me everything."

As they recounted their journey and the discovery of the relic, Father Miguel listened intently, his expression thoughtful. When they finished, he leaned back in his chair, his eyes closed in contemplation.

"The relic you have found is indeed of great importance," Father Miguel began, opening his eyes. "It is a symbol of faith and protection, used by early Christians during times of great peril. But it is more than that. It holds a power that can be used for both good and evil."

Emily leaned forward, her eyes wide with curiosity. "What kind of power?"

Father Miguel sighed. "The relic was believed to be blessed, capable of healing and protection. But in the wrong hands, it can also be a tool of destruction. That is why it was hidden away, protected by those who understood its true nature."

Reed nodded. "We've faced attacks from a cult led by Anton Graves. He believes the relic can grant him supernatural powers. We need to know how to protect it and ensure it doesn't fall into his hands."

Father Miguel's expression darkened. "Anton Graves is a dangerous man. His intentions are twisted, driven by a lust for power. You must be vigilant and steadfast in your mission."

Gabriel, who had been silent until now, spoke up. "Father, is there a way to neutralize the relic's power, to make it useless to Graves?"

Father Miguel shook his head. "The power of the relic cannot be neutralized. But it can be safeguarded. The sanctuary where you found it is designed to protect it, but there are other measures that can be taken."

"Such as?" Emily asked, her voice filled with determination.

"There are ancient rituals and protections that can be invoked," Father Miguel explained. "But they require great faith and purity of heart. I can teach you these rituals, but you must be committed to using them for the right reasons."

Reed exchanged a glance with Emily and Gabriel. "We are committed. We'll do whatever it takes to protect the relic."

Father Miguel smiled, a look of approval in his eyes. "Very well. We will begin the teachings tomorrow. For now, rest and regain your strength. You have a long journey ahead."

The next morning, the team gathered in a small chapel within the monastery, the air filled with the scent of incense and the soft glow of candlelight. Father Miguel stood at the altar, his presence commanding and serene.

"Before we begin," Father Miguel said, "you must understand that these rituals are not merely words or actions. They are a manifestation of faith and intention. You must believe in their power and in your purpose."

Reed nodded, his expression serious. "We understand, Father."

"Good," Father Miguel replied. "Now, let us begin."

He led them through a series of prayers and rituals, each one designed to invoke protection and strength. Emily, Reed, and Gabriel followed his instructions carefully, their hearts and minds focused on the task at hand.

As they practiced, Father Miguel shared stories of the early Christians who had used these same rituals to protect themselves and their communities. His words were filled with wisdom and inspiration, a reminder of the strength and resilience of those who had come before them.

"These rituals are a legacy," Father Miguel said, his voice echoing in the chapel. "They have been passed down through generations, a testament to the enduring power of faith. You are now part of that legacy. Use it wisely."

By the end of the day, they had mastered the basics of the rituals. They felt a renewed sense of purpose and determination, bolstered by Father

Miguel's guidance and the knowledge that they were not alone in their mission.

As evening fell, they gathered in the courtyard, the cool mountain air a welcome relief after the intense day. Father Miguel joined them, his presence a comforting beacon of wisdom and strength.

"Father," Reed began, "we can't thank you enough for your guidance. You've given us the tools we need to protect the relic. But we still have so many questions."

Father Miguel nodded, his expression understanding. "I will answer what I can. What do you wish to know?"

Emily spoke up. "The sanctuary and the relic—why were they hidden? What were the early Christians protecting them from?"

Father Miguel's eyes grew distant as he considered her question. "The sanctuary was built during a time of great persecution. The early Christians were hunted, their faith seen as a threat to the established order. They created sanctuaries like the one you found as places of refuge and protection, both for themselves and for their sacred artifacts."

"And the relic?" Gabriel asked. "What is its true purpose?"

"The relic is a symbol of divine protection," Father Miguel explained. "It was believed to be blessed by God, a source of strength and healing for those who possessed it. But its power is also a responsibility. Those who seek to misuse it for their own gain will find that it brings only destruction."

Reed's expression grew serious. "Anton Graves believes he can use the relic to gain supernatural powers. How do we stop him?"

Father Miguel's eyes hardened. "Graves is blinded by his ambition. He sees only the power, not the responsibility. You must use the rituals I have taught you to protect the relic. Keep it hidden and guarded, and do not let it fall into his hands."

Emily nodded, her resolve firm. "We will. We won't let him take it."

Father Miguel smiled, a look of pride in his eyes. "I believe in you. You have the strength and faith to see this through. Remember, you are not alone. The legacy of those who came before you is with you, guiding you."

The next morning, they prepared to leave the monastery, their hearts filled with gratitude and determination. Father Miguel stood at the entrance, his eyes filled with a quiet strength.

"Thank you, Father," Reed said, bowing his head in respect. "We won't forget your guidance."

"Go with God," Father Miguel replied, his voice gentle. "And remember, the true power of the relic lies not in its physical form, but in the faith and strength of those who protect it."

As they set off down the mountain, the monastery slowly fading from view, they felt a renewed sense of purpose. They had the knowledge and the tools to protect the relic, and they were ready to face whatever challenges lay ahead.

"We have a long journey ahead," Reed said, his voice filled with determination. "But we're not alone. We have each other, and we have the legacy of those who came before us."

Emily nodded, her eyes shining with resolve. "We'll protect the relic. No matter what."

Gabriel grinned, his usual humor shining through. "Let's get to it, then. Graves won't know what hit him."

As they continued their journey, they felt a sense of unity and strength. They were not just protectors of the relic; they were part of a legacy that spanned centuries, a testament to the enduring power of faith and resilience.

And they were ready to face whatever trials lay ahead, together.

7

Pursuit Begins

The desert stretched endlessly before them, a vast expanse of shifting sands and rocky outcrops. Dr. Jonathan Reed, Emily Carter, and Gabriel Martinez moved with a renewed sense of purpose, their mission clear and their resolve unshakable. They had left the safety of Father Miguel's monastery behind, but his wisdom and guidance traveled with them, a comforting presence in their minds.

"We need to keep moving," Reed said, his eyes scanning the horizon. "Graves and his followers won't be far behind."

Emily adjusted the strap of her backpack, her gaze focused. "We have to reach the next site before they do. The hidden chamber Father Miguel mentioned is our best chance to understand and protect the relic."

Gabriel, ever the pragmatist, nodded. "And we need to stay vigilant. Graves will stop at nothing to get what he wants."

They pressed on, their footsteps leaving a trail in the sand that the wind quickly erased. The heat was oppressive, but they moved with determination, knowing that every moment counted.

By late afternoon, they reached a series of ancient ruins partially buried in the sand. The structures, though weathered by time, still stood as silent sentinels over the desert landscape. Reed paused, studying the layout of the ruins with a keen eye.

"This is it," he said, pointing to a crumbling archway. "The entrance to the hidden chamber should be through there."

Emily and Gabriel followed him, their movements cautious but purposeful. The air grew cooler as they entered the ruins, the sun's harsh rays blocked by the ancient stone walls.

"We need to find the mechanism Father Miguel mentioned," Emily said, her voice echoing slightly in the narrow passageway. "It's the key to accessing the hidden chamber."

Gabriel scanned the walls, his eyes sharp. "Look for anything that seems out of place. A symbol, a lever, anything."

They spread out, each examining different sections of the passageway. After a few minutes, Reed called out.

"Over here. I think I've found something."

Emily and Gabriel joined him, peering at a series of carvings on the wall. The symbols were intricate and faint, but their meaning was clear.

"It's a riddle," Emily said, translating the ancient script. "'When light meets shadow, the path will be revealed.'"

Gabriel frowned. "Light and shadow? What does that mean?"

Reed thought for a moment, then looked up at a small opening in the ceiling. "The light from the setting sun. It must cast a shadow that points the way."

"We need to time this perfectly," Emily said. "Let's wait and see where the shadow falls."

They waited in tense silence as the sun dipped lower in the sky. As the light shifted, a shadow began to form, creeping slowly across the floor. It moved toward a seemingly solid wall, stopping at a specific point.

"There," Reed said, moving quickly to the spot. He pressed against the wall, and with a soft rumble, a hidden door slid open, revealing a dark passageway.

"Nice work," Gabriel said, clapping Reed on the back.

Reed smiled. "Let's see what's inside."

They entered the passageway, their flashlights cutting through the darkness. The air was cool and damp, the walls lined with more intricate carvings. As they moved deeper, the passage opened into a large chamber.

In the center of the chamber stood a stone altar, upon which rested an ancient, ornate box. Emily approached it cautiously, her heart pounding with anticipation.

"This must be it," she whispered. "The hidden chamber."

Reed and Gabriel joined her, their eyes wide with awe. "Let's open it," Reed said softly.

Emily carefully lifted the lid, revealing a collection of scrolls and a small, intricately carved statue. "These scrolls could provide the answers we've been looking for," she said, her voice filled with excitement.

Gabriel examined the statue. "And this... it looks like it's part of a larger set. We need to figure out its significance."

Reed nodded. "Let's document everything and get out of here. We don't know how much time we have before Graves catches up with us."

As they exited the chamber, the sun had nearly set, casting long shadows over the ruins. The sense of urgency was palpable, and they moved quickly, packing up their findings and preparing to leave.

But as they made their way back through the ruins, a sudden noise made them freeze. Footsteps, heavy and deliberate, echoed through the passageway.

"Graves," Gabriel whispered, his hand moving to the hilt of his knife. "He's here."

Reed's mind raced. "We need to get out of here. Now."

They moved swiftly but quietly, sticking to the shadows as they made their way toward the entrance. The sound of footsteps grew louder, closer, until they could hear the low murmur of voices.

"Keep moving," Reed urged, his voice barely audible.

They reached the entrance just as Graves and his followers came into view, their dark forms silhouetted against the fading light. Graves' eyes locked onto Reed's, a cold smile spreading across his face.

"Going somewhere, Dr. Reed?" Graves called out, his voice dripping with malice.

Reed didn't respond. He motioned for Emily and Gabriel to keep moving, his eyes never leaving Graves.

"Get them," Graves ordered, and his followers surged forward.

The chase was on. Reed, Emily, and Gabriel sprinted through the ruins, their hearts pounding. The uneven ground and crumbling structures made the escape treacherous, but they pushed forward, driven by the need to protect the relic and their lives.

"This way!" Gabriel shouted, leading them toward a narrow alley between two ancient walls.

They ducked into the alley, the walls pressing in on them. The sound of their pursuers' footsteps echoed behind them, growing closer with each passing moment.

"We need to split up," Reed said urgently. "It's our best chance."

Emily hesitated. "But—"

"No time," Reed interrupted. "Go! We'll meet at the next waypoint."

Reluctantly, Emily nodded. She took off down a side passage, her footsteps light and swift. Reed and Gabriel continued straight, their path fraught with obstacles.

Graves' men were relentless, their dark forms closing in. Reed and Gabriel pushed themselves to the limit, navigating the ruins with a desperate agility.

"Up here!" Gabriel shouted, pointing to a crumbling staircase.

They ascended quickly, the ancient stone steps crumbling beneath their feet. At the top, they found a narrow ledge that led to another part of the ruins.

"Careful," Reed cautioned, moving along the ledge.

They reached the other side, but the sound of pursuit was still close. Reed looked around, searching for an escape route.

"There," he said, pointing to a narrow gap in the wall. "We can squeeze through and lose them in the maze of passages beyond."

They moved quickly, slipping through the gap just as Graves and his men arrived at the ledge. For a moment, it seemed they might escape.

But then, a sharp voice cut through the air. "There they are!"

Reed and Gabriel ducked into the maze of passages, their hearts pounding. They could hear Graves' men behind them, the sound of their pursuit growing louder.

"We need to find Emily," Reed said, his voice tight with urgency.

Gabriel nodded. "She should be heading toward the waypoint."

They moved through the maze with practiced speed, their familiarity with the ruins giving them an edge. But the relentless pursuit made it clear that they couldn't stay hidden forever.

Meanwhile, Emily navigated the ruins with a combination of speed and stealth. She could hear the sound of footsteps behind her, but she focused on her path, her mind sharp and clear.

She reached the waypoint, a small, hidden alcove that they had designated as a meeting point. She pressed herself against the wall, trying to control her breathing as she listened for any sign of Reed and Gabriel.

Minutes passed, each one feeling like an eternity. Finally, she heard the sound of approaching footsteps—Reed and Gabriel's voices, urgent but controlled.

"Emily?" Reed called out softly.

"Here," she replied, stepping out from the shadows.

Reed and Gabriel joined her, their expressions a mix of relief and determination.

"We need to keep moving," Gabriel said. "Graves' men are right behind us."

Emily nodded. "Let's go."

They moved quickly, sticking to the shadows as they made their way through the ruins. The sense of urgency was palpable, the knowledge that Graves was so close adding a sharp edge to their movements.

The night deepened, the ruins cast in a ghostly light as the moon rose. Reed, Emily, and Gabriel continued their escape, their breath coming in short bursts as they navigated the ancient passages.

"We're almost there," Reed said, his voice tight with determination. "Just a little farther."

But as they rounded a corner, they found themselves face to face with a group of Graves' men, their eyes cold and unyielding.

"Well, well," one of the men sneered. "Looks like we've got you cornered."

Reed's mind raced. "We don't have to do this," he said, trying to buy time. "You don't understand the significance of the relic. It's not just a source of power."

The man's expression hardened. "Save your breath, Reed. We know exactly what we're after."

Before Reed could respond, Gabriel lunged at the nearest man, his movements swift and precise. The ruins erupted into chaos as they fought, the sound of blows and grunts echoing through the passageway.

Emily fought with a fierce determination, her mind focused on protecting the relic. She dodged a punch and countered with a swift kick, her movements fluid and controlled.

Reed joined the fray, his years of field experience giving him an edge. He fought with a combination of strength and strategy, using the environment to his advantage.

The battle was intense, but they were outnumbered. Reed, Emily, and Gabriel fought valiantly, but it was clear that they couldn't hold out forever.

Just as hope began to wane, a voice rang out from the shadows. "Enough!"

The fighting stopped as everyone turned to see a tall, imposing figure step into the light—Anton Graves himself.

"Dr. Reed," Graves said, his voice smooth and menacing. "I must admit, you've given us quite the chase. But it ends here."

Reed's eyes narrowed. "You're making a mistake, Graves. The relic isn't what you think it is."

Graves smiled, a cold, calculated expression. "On the contrary, Reed. I know exactly what it is. And I intend to use it to reshape the world."

Emily stepped forward, her eyes blazing with determination. "You won't succeed, Graves. We won't let you."

Graves chuckled. "Brave words, Ms. Carter. But words won't save you."

With a swift motion, Graves' men moved forward, grabbing Reed, Emily, and Gabriel. Despite their struggles, they were quickly overpowered and restrained.

Graves approached, his eyes gleaming with triumph. "The relic is mine, Reed. And there's nothing you can do to stop me."

Reed met his gaze, his expression defiant. "This isn't over, Graves. We'll stop you. No matter what."

Graves' smile widened. "We'll see about that."

As they were led away, the weight of their situation settled heavily upon them. They had come so far, uncovered so much, but now they faced their greatest challenge yet. The fight to protect the relic and the legacy of those who had come before them was far from over.

But even in the face of despair, their resolve remained unbroken. They had each other, and they had the strength and faith to see this through. And they knew that, no matter what, they would fight to the end.

As they were taken deeper into the ruins, Reed, Emily, and Gabriel exchanged determined looks. They knew the risks, but they also knew their mission was too important to abandon.

"We'll find a way," Reed whispered, his voice filled with conviction. "We won't let Graves win."

Emily nodded, her eyes shining with resolve. "We'll protect the relic. No matter what it takes."

Gabriel grinned, his usual humor shining through even in the darkest moments. "Let's give them hell."

As they faced the uncertain future, they knew one thing for sure: their journey was far from over, and they were ready to face whatever challenges lay ahead, together.

8

The Hidden Chamber

The air was thick with tension as Dr. Jonathan Reed, Emily Carter, and Gabriel Martinez were led deeper into the ruins by Graves' men. The narrow passages seemed to close in around them, the flickering torchlight casting eerie shadows on the ancient walls. The sense of urgency and danger was palpable, but their resolve remained unbroken.

Anton Graves walked ahead, his posture exuding confidence and authority. He glanced back at his captives with a cold smile. "You've put up quite a fight, but it's over now. The relic will be mine."

Reed met Graves' gaze with defiance. "You're making a mistake, Graves. You don't understand the true nature of the relic."

Graves chuckled, his eyes gleaming with ambition. "On the contrary, Reed. I understand it perfectly. And I intend to harness its power."

Emily's eyes blazed with determination. "We won't let you."

Graves ignored her, leading them into a large, dimly lit chamber. The room was dominated by an imposing altar, upon which the relic now rested. The atmosphere was charged with an almost tangible energy, the air crackling with the relic's latent power.

Gabriel's eyes scanned the room, taking in the ancient symbols etched into the walls. "This place... it's like the heart of the sanctuary. The epicenter of its power."

Graves approached the altar, his fingers hovering just above the relic. "This is it," he murmured, more to himself than to his followers. "This is the key to everything."

Reed, Emily, and Gabriel exchanged a look. They knew they had to act, and they had to act fast.

Reed's mind raced. "Graves, listen to me. The relic's power is not just a tool. It's a responsibility. Misusing it could have catastrophic consequences."

Graves turned to face him, a sneer on his lips. "You think I don't know that? I'm willing to take that risk. The world needs to be reshaped, and I have the vision to do it."

Emily stepped forward, her voice firm. "You're blinded by your ambition, Graves. The relic's true power lies in faith and protection, not in domination."

Graves' expression hardened. "Enough. Take them away."

His men moved to comply, roughly grabbing Reed, Emily, and Gabriel. But as they were led toward the exit, a sudden noise echoed through the chamber—a deep, resonant hum that seemed to emanate from the very walls.

Graves turned back to the altar, his eyes widening in surprise. "What's happening?"

The relic began to glow, its light growing brighter and more intense. The symbols on the walls pulsed with energy, responding to the relic's activation.

Reed seized the moment. "This is our chance!" he shouted.

Gabriel reacted first, elbowing the guard holding him and breaking free. He lunged for another guard, taking him down with a swift, practiced move. Emily followed suit, using the distraction to break away and grab a weapon from one of the fallen guards.

Reed moved toward Graves, his eyes fixed on the glowing relic. "Stop this, Graves! You don't know what you're unleashing!"

Graves hesitated, his eyes flicking between the relic and Reed. For a moment, doubt crossed his face, but it was quickly replaced by steely determination. "I won't let you stop me."

With a sudden movement, Graves reached out and grasped the relic. The light flared blindingly bright, and a shockwave of energy rippled through the chamber, throwing everyone off their feet.

When the light faded, the chamber was filled with an eerie silence. Reed struggled to his feet, his vision swimming. He saw Emily and Gabriel nearby, both slowly getting up, their faces etched with concern.

"Jonathan, are you okay?" Emily asked, her voice shaky.

Reed nodded, trying to shake off the dizziness. "I'm fine. What about Graves?"

Gabriel pointed to the altar, where Graves stood, his body surrounded by a shimmering aura. His eyes were wide with shock and pain, his grip on the relic unsteady.

"Graves!" Reed called out. "Let go of the relic! You're not in control!"

Graves' voice was a strained whisper. "I... I can feel its power... it's too much..."

Emily moved toward him, her hands outstretched. "You have to let go, Graves. It's not meant to be used this way."

Graves' expression twisted with fear and desperation. "No... I can't... I have to..."

Before he could finish, the relic's light flared again, and another shockwave pulsed through the chamber. Graves cried out in agony, his body convulsing as the relic's power overwhelmed him.

Reed rushed forward, grabbing Graves and pulling him away from the altar. The relic fell from his grasp, its light dimming as it hit the ground.

Gabriel quickly retrieved the relic, wrapping it in a cloth to contain its power. "We need to get out of here. This place is unstable."

Reed supported Graves, who was barely conscious, and they made their way toward the exit. The chamber trembled, the ancient stones cracking and shifting as the relic's energy destabilized the structure.

Outside the ruins, the cool night air was a stark contrast to the intense heat and energy inside. They moved quickly, putting distance between themselves and the crumbling ruins.

Reed laid Graves down gently, checking his pulse. "He's alive, but we need to get him medical attention."

Emily knelt beside them, her face filled with concern. "What do we do now? The relic is too powerful to be left unguarded."

Gabriel looked around, his expression serious. "We need to hide it somewhere safe. Somewhere Graves and his followers can't find it."

Reed nodded. "Father Miguel mentioned other sanctuaries. Places that were designed to protect artifacts like this. We need to find one."

Emily stood, determination in her eyes. "Then let's go. We can't afford to waste any time."

As they prepared to leave, Reed glanced back at the ruins, the weight of their mission pressing heavily on his shoulders. They had come so far and uncovered so much, but the real challenge was just beginning.

They traveled through the night, their pace steady and determined. Graves was unconscious, but stable, carried on a makeshift stretcher. They moved quickly, knowing that they couldn't afford to be caught out in the open.

As dawn broke, they reached a small village nestled in the mountains. The villagers greeted them with cautious curiosity, but were quick to offer help when they saw Graves' condition.

"We need a place to rest and tend to our friend," Reed explained to the village elder, a kind-faced woman with a weathered appearance.

The elder nodded. "You're welcome here. We have a healer who can help. Come, follow me."

They were led to a small, cozy hut where the healer, an elderly man with a gentle demeanor, quickly set to work on Graves. The team watched anxiously, knowing that their mission hinged on Graves' condition and their ability to stay ahead of his followers.

As the healer worked, Reed, Emily, and Gabriel discussed their next steps.

"We need to find another sanctuary," Emily said. "One that's hidden and secure."

Reed nodded. "Father Miguel mentioned a place in the northern mountains. It's remote and difficult to reach, but it's our best option."

Gabriel looked at the relic, still wrapped in the cloth. "We need to be careful. Even hidden, the relic's power could attract attention."

Reed agreed. "We'll have to be discreet. Only a few people can know about this."

The healer approached them, his expression reassuring. "Your friend will recover. He needs rest, but he'll be fine."

"Thank you," Reed said, his relief evident. "We appreciate your help."

The elder, who had been listening quietly, spoke up. "You carry a heavy burden. If there is anything else we can do to help, please let us know."

Emily smiled gratefully. "Just a safe place to rest for a while. And perhaps some guidance on the best route to the northern mountains."

The elder nodded. "You are welcome to stay as long as you need. And I will send for someone who knows the mountains well. They will guide you."

Over the next few days, they rested and prepared for the journey ahead. Graves regained consciousness, his condition improving steadily. Though still weak, he was coherent and aware of the gravity of his situation.

Reed sat by Graves' bedside, their expressions serious. "Graves, you need to understand the danger of what you were trying to do. The relic is not a tool for power."

Graves' eyes were filled with a mix of regret and determination. "I thought I could control it. I thought... I could change things for the better."

Emily joined them, her voice gentle but firm. "The relic's power is not meant to be controlled. It's a responsibility, one that we must protect."

Graves nodded slowly. "I see that now. I was blinded by my ambition. I'm sorry for what I've done."

Reed placed a hand on his shoulder. "What's important now is that we protect the relic. We need your help, Graves. You know more about the cult and their plans than anyone."

Graves took a deep breath, his resolve strengthening. "I'll help you. I owe you that much."

Gabriel entered the hut, his expression serious. "Our guide has arrived. We should leave soon."

Reed nodded. "We're ready."

The journey to the northern mountains was grueling. The terrain was rugged and unforgiving, but their guide, a weathered mountaineer named Tomas, led them with expert precision. They moved carefully, aware that they could be pursued at any moment.

"We need to stay off the main paths," Tomas advised. "The cult could have scouts in the area."

Emily looked up at the towering peaks ahead. "How much farther?"

Tomas pointed to a distant ridge. "Not far now. The sanctuary is hidden in a cave system near the summit."

Reed nodded. "We'll need to move quickly. Once we reach the sanctuary, we can set up defenses and ensure the relic is secure."

As they climbed higher, the air grew thinner and colder. The sense of urgency and danger was ever-present, but they pressed on, driven by their mission.

Finally, they reached the entrance to the cave system. It was well hidden, the narrow opening concealed by thick underbrush and rocks.

Tomas led them inside, the cave opening up into a series of interconnected chambers. "This is it," he said. "The sanctuary lies deeper within."

They moved through the caves, their flashlights casting eerie shadows on the walls. The sense of history and sanctity was palpable, the air thick with the weight of centuries.

In the innermost chamber, they found an ancient altar, similar to the one they had seen before. The symbols on the walls glowed faintly, a testament to the power that lay within.

Reed placed the relic on the altar, his expression filled with a mix of reverence and determination. "We've done it. The relic is safe."

Emily and Gabriel joined him, their faces etched with relief and resolve. They knew their journey was far from over, but they had taken a crucial step in protecting the relic and the legacy it represented.

Graves stood at the entrance to the chamber, his eyes filled with a newfound respect for the power and responsibility they had undertaken. "Thank you," he said quietly. "For giving me a chance to make things right."

Reed nodded. "We're all in this together. We'll protect the relic, and we'll stop the cult. No matter what."

As they prepared to defend the sanctuary and continue their mission, they felt a renewed sense of unity and purpose. They had come so far, and they were ready to face whatever challenges lay ahead.

Together, they would protect the relic and the legacy of those who had come before them. And they would ensure that its power was used for good, not for destruction.

9

Escape and Reflection

The hidden sanctuary provided a temporary refuge, but the weight of their mission pressed heavily on Dr. Jonathan Reed, Emily Carter, Gabriel Martinez, and even the now-repentant Anton Graves. The ancient cave system, with its intricate carvings and ethereal glow, felt both sacred and somber, a testament to the countless souls who had sought protection here.

Reed stood before the ancient altar, the relic safely ensconced within its protective casing. The air was thick with the scent of incense, remnants from rituals performed by guardians long since gone. He turned to his companions, their faces illuminated by the flickering torchlight.

"We can't stay here forever," Reed said, his voice echoing in the cavernous chamber. "Graves' followers will eventually find us. We need a plan to keep the relic safe and continue our mission."

Gabriel, ever the pragmatist, nodded. "Agreed. But we also need to rest and regroup. We've been running non-stop."

Emily looked thoughtful. "What about contacting Father Miguel again? He might have more advice on where to go next, or how to better protect the relic."

Graves, sitting quietly by the chamber's entrance, spoke up. "I know I'm not in a position to demand anything, but I have information on the cult's movements. They have resources and contacts that could make hiding difficult. We need to think strategically."

Reed nodded, appreciating Graves' willingness to help. "Alright, let's rest for now. In the morning, we'll reach out to Father Miguel and formulate a plan."

As the team settled into the sanctuary for the night, the atmosphere was a mix of exhaustion and determination. The flickering fire cast long shadows on the walls, creating an almost mystical ambiance. Emily sat by the fire, her eyes reflecting the dancing flames, deep in thought.

Gabriel joined her, handing over a cup of tea. "Penny for your thoughts?"

Emily smiled, taking the cup. "Just thinking about how far we've come, and how much farther we have to go. This mission... it feels like it's about more than just the relic."

Gabriel nodded. "It is. It's about faith, history, and protecting something much bigger than ourselves. But we'll get through it. Together."

Emily looked around the chamber, taking in the sight of her companions. "I'm glad we're in this together. I couldn't ask for a better team."

Reed approached, sitting down beside them. "Neither could I. We've faced incredible challenges, and we've come out stronger each time."

Graves, from his spot by the entrance, added quietly, "I've spent so much time chasing power, I forgot what true strength looks like. Watching you all... it's been humbling."

Reed gave him a reassuring nod. "Everyone makes mistakes, Graves. What matters is that you're here now, willing to help. We'll need all the help we can get."

The next morning, the team contacted Father Miguel using a satellite phone. His calm, steady voice provided a much-needed sense of reassurance.

"Father Miguel, we've reached the sanctuary and secured the relic," Reed began. "But we know we can't stay here indefinitely. Do you have any advice on where we should go next?"

Father Miguel's voice crackled through the line. "I'm glad to hear you're safe. There are other sanctuaries, but the key lies not just in location, but in the safeguards you set. You must use the rituals I taught you to protect the relic."

Emily nodded, even though Father Miguel couldn't see her. "We understand, Father. But how do we ensure that Graves' followers can't find us again?"

"There is a place," Father Miguel replied, "an ancient monastery hidden deep within the mountains, far from any civilization. It's a place of great power and protection. Go there, and perform the rituals. It will help shield the relic from those with ill intentions."

Reed exchanged glances with his team. "Thank you, Father. We'll head there immediately. We appreciate your guidance."

"May God be with you," Father Miguel said before the line went dead.

The journey to the ancient monastery was long and treacherous, taking them through rugged mountain passes and dense forests. The further they traveled, the more isolated they became, the sense of remoteness adding to the gravity of their mission.

As they neared the monastery, the landscape became even more challenging, with steep cliffs and narrow paths that required careful navigation. But the team pressed on, their determination unwavering.

Finally, after days of arduous travel, they arrived at the hidden monastery. It was a magnificent structure, carved into the mountainside, with towering spires and intricate stonework that spoke of its ancient origins.

"This place is incredible," Gabriel said, awe evident in his voice. "It's like something out of a legend."

Emily nodded, her eyes wide with wonder. "I can feel the power here. It's like the very air is charged with it."

Reed approached the massive wooden doors, pushing them open with a sense of reverence. Inside, the monastery was just as awe-inspiring, with vaulted ceilings, stained glass windows, and an air of sanctity that seemed to permeate every corner.

"We need to perform the rituals Father Miguel taught us," Reed said, his voice echoing in the vast hall. "Let's get to work."

The team spent the next several hours preparing the rituals, setting up altars and lighting candles in the designated areas. Emily, with her deep knowledge of early Christian practices, led the ceremonies, her voice steady and filled with conviction.

As they chanted the ancient prayers and performed the intricate rituals, the air around them seemed to vibrate with energy. The symbols on the walls glowed faintly, responding to their invocations, and a sense of peace and protection settled over the monastery.

"This feels right," Emily said, her voice barely above a whisper. "We're doing exactly what needs to be done."

Gabriel nodded. "I can feel it too. This place is a fortress of faith."

Reed stood by the altar, the relic safely secured within its protective casing. "We've done everything we can. Now, we need to trust in the power of these rituals and in our ability to protect the relic."

That night, as they sat around a small fire in the monastery's courtyard, the weight of their journey began to lift slightly. The stars above them twinkled brightly, and the cool mountain air was refreshing after the intense heat of the desert.

Graves, who had been quiet for much of the day, finally spoke. "I want to thank you all. For giving me a chance to make amends. I know I have a long way to go, but I'm committed to helping you protect the relic."

Reed looked at him, his expression serious but compassionate. "Redemption is a journey, Graves. What matters is that you're willing to walk it."

Emily added, "We believe in second chances. And we'll need all the help we can get to keep the relic safe."

Gabriel raised his cup in a toast. "To new allies, and to protecting the legacy we've been entrusted with."

They clinked their cups together, the sound echoing in the still night air. For the first time in a long while, they allowed themselves a moment of peace, knowing that their mission was far from over, but confident in their ability to see it through.

The following days were spent fortifying the monastery and further familiarizing themselves with its layout and history. The ancient structure held many secrets, and the team worked diligently to uncover and understand them.

Reed and Emily spent hours poring over ancient texts and inscriptions, their knowledge of early Christian history proving invaluable. Gabriel focused on reinforcing the physical defenses of the monastery, ensuring that they were prepared for any potential attacks.

Graves, true to his word, shared everything he knew about the cult's movements and plans. His insider knowledge proved crucial in anticipating potential threats and staying one step ahead of their enemies.

One evening, as the team gathered in the monastery's library, Graves shared a particularly troubling piece of information.

"I've heard rumors," he began, his voice low, "that the cult is planning a major offensive. They're gathering resources and followers from all over, preparing for a final push to take the relic."

Reed's expression grew serious. "Do you know when and where they plan to strike?"

Graves shook his head. "Not exactly. But I know they're desperate. They'll stop at nothing to get what they want."

Emily's eyes flashed with determination. "Then we need to be ready. We need to fortify this place and ensure the relic is as protected as possible."

Gabriel nodded in agreement. "We'll set up additional defenses and prepare for the worst. We've come too far to let the relic fall into their hands."

The days that followed were filled with intense preparation. The team worked tirelessly to strengthen the monastery's defenses, setting traps, securing entrances, and ensuring that the relic was well-protected.

Emily led them in regular rituals, reinforcing the protective barriers around the relic and the monastery. The sense of unity and purpose that had brought them this far was stronger than ever, and they knew that they were ready to face whatever challenges lay ahead.

One evening, as they sat around the fire, Reed spoke up, his voice filled with a quiet determination. "We've done everything we can to prepare. Now, we need to trust in each other and in the power of the rituals we've performed."

Emily nodded, her eyes reflecting the flickering flames. "We're ready. Whatever comes, we'll face it together."

Gabriel raised his cup in a toast. "To the journey ahead, and to protecting the legacy we've been entrusted with."

Graves, his expression serious but hopeful, added, "To redemption, and to doing what's right."

They clinked their cups together, the sound echoing in the still night air. For a moment, they allowed themselves to feel a sense of peace, knowing that they had done everything in their power to protect the relic and prepare for the battle that was sure to come.

As they sat together, the weight of their mission pressing heavily on their shoulders, they knew that the road ahead would be difficult and dangerous. But they also knew that they were not alone. They had each other, and they had the strength and faith to see their mission through to the end.

In the quiet moments before dawn, Reed stood by the altar, the relic glowing faintly within its protective casing. He closed his eyes, his thoughts a prayer for strength and guidance.

"We're ready," he whispered. "Whatever comes, we'll face it. Together."

The first light of dawn began to filter through the monastery's stained glass windows, casting a soft glow over the ancient stone walls. Reed took a deep breath, feeling a renewed sense of purpose and determination.

The battle to protect the relic and the legacy of those who had come before them was far from over. But they were ready to face it, united by their shared mission and their unwavering faith.

As the sun rose, casting its light over the mountains, the team prepared for the challenges ahead. They knew that they were not just fighting for themselves, but for a cause much greater than any one of them.

And with that knowledge, they felt a sense of peace and resolve, ready to face whatever trials lay ahead, together.

10

The Battle for the Relic

The tranquility of the ancient monastery was a stark contrast to the tension that permeated the air. Dr. Jonathan Reed, Emily Carter, Gabriel Martinez, and Anton Graves knew that their peace was fragile. Graves' intelligence had confirmed their worst fears—the cult was planning a major offensive. As they fortified the monastery and prepared for the inevitable clash, a sense of grim determination settled over the group.

Reed gathered his team in the central hall, the relic securely placed on the altar behind them. The symbols on the walls seemed to pulse with a faint light, a silent testament to the power and history within these ancient stones.

"We've done everything we can to prepare," Reed began, his voice steady. "Now we need to stay vigilant. Graves, do you have any more details on their plans?"

Graves shook his head, his expression serious. "All I know is that they're coming, and they're coming soon. We need to be ready for anything."

Gabriel, ever the pragmatist, spoke up. "We've reinforced the entrances and set up traps. Emily's rituals have strengthened the protective barriers. But we can't afford to be complacent."

Emily nodded, her eyes reflecting her determination. "We need to be ready to fight. But we also need to protect the relic. It's our primary responsibility."

Reed placed a hand on the altar, feeling the faint warmth emanating from the relic. "We'll protect it. No matter what."

The first signs of the impending attack came at dawn. A distant rumble echoed through the mountains, growing steadily louder. The team gathered in the central hall, their expressions a mix of determination and resolve.

"They're coming," Gabriel said, his voice low.

Reed nodded. "Everyone, take your positions. Remember, our primary goal is to protect the relic."

They moved quickly, each taking their assigned posts. Gabriel manned the main entrance, his eyes scanning the horizon for any sign of movement. Emily and Graves positioned themselves near the secondary entrances, ready to defend against any intruders.

Reed stayed in the central hall, his gaze fixed on the relic. The air was thick with anticipation, the silence broken only by the distant rumble of approaching footsteps.

Suddenly, a loud crash echoed through the monastery as the cult's forces breached the outer defenses. The battle had begun.

Gabriel was the first to engage, his movements swift and precise as he fought off the attackers at the main entrance. "They're here!" he shouted, his voice carrying through the halls. "Everyone, hold your ground!"

Emily and Graves responded quickly, fending off the intruders at their respective posts. The sound of clashing weapons and shouted commands filled the air, the once serene monastery now a battleground.

Reed remained by the altar, his heart pounding as he watched the chaos unfold. He knew he needed to stay focused, to protect the relic at all costs. But the sight of his friends fighting so fiercely filled him with a mix of pride and fear.

"Jonathan!" Emily's voice rang out, sharp and urgent. "We need backup at the secondary entrance!"

Reed grabbed a weapon and rushed to Emily's side, joining the fray. The attackers were relentless, their eyes filled with a fanatical intensity. But Emily and Reed fought with a determination born of necessity, their movements synchronized and efficient.

"We can't let them through!" Reed shouted, deflecting a blow aimed at Emily. "Hold the line!"

Emily nodded, her expression fierce. "We won't let them take the relic. No matter what."

Meanwhile, Gabriel was holding his ground at the main entrance, his strength and agility keeping the attackers at bay. But he knew they couldn't keep this up forever.

"Graves!" Gabriel called out. "How are you holding up?"

Graves, fighting near another entrance, responded through gritted teeth. "We're managing, but they keep coming. We need to find a way to turn the tide."

Gabriel's mind raced. "We need to regroup and push them back. Emily, can you reinforce the protective barriers?"

Emily, still fighting fiercely, shouted back. "I can try, but I need cover!"

Reed, overhearing the exchange, nodded. "Gabriel, you and Graves hold the entrances. I'll cover Emily."

Gabriel and Graves moved to fortify their positions as Reed and Emily worked together. Emily began chanting the protective rituals, her voice steady despite the chaos around her. Reed stood guard, fending off any attackers that tried to interrupt her.

As Emily's voice rose, the symbols on the walls began to glow brighter, the protective barriers strengthening. The cultists hesitated, their movements faltering as the power of the rituals took hold.

"It's working!" Emily shouted, her voice filled with hope. "Keep them at bay a little longer!"

Reed fought with renewed vigor, his movements precise and controlled. "We can do this! Just a little longer!"

The battle raged on, the cultists relentless in their pursuit of the relic. But the team's unity and determination began to turn the tide. Gabriel and Graves held their ground, their strength and strategy keeping the attackers at bay.

Emily's rituals created a protective barrier around the relic, the symbols on the walls glowing with an almost blinding light. The cultists, sensing the growing power of the rituals, grew more desperate and frenzied.

"We need to hold them off until the rituals are complete!" Reed shouted, his voice carrying through the chaos.

Gabriel responded with a fierce determination. "We won't let them through! Not while we're here!"

Graves, fighting with a newfound purpose, added, "We protect the relic. Together."

As the battle reached its peak, the cultists made one final, desperate push. Their leader, a tall, imposing figure with a scarred face, advanced toward the central hall, his eyes fixed on the relic.

"Stop him!" Reed shouted, his voice filled with urgency.

Gabriel and Graves moved to intercept, their movements swift and coordinated. They fought with a fierce determination, their combined strength and skill overwhelming the cult leader.

"You will not take the relic!" Gabriel shouted, his voice echoing through the hall.

The cult leader sneered, his eyes filled with malice. "You think you can stop me? The relic's power will be mine!"

Graves, his expression resolute, responded, "Not while we're here."

With a final, coordinated effort, Gabriel and Graves disarmed the cult leader, their combined strength bringing him to his knees. The remaining cultists, seeing their leader defeated, began to retreat, their fanatical resolve broken.

As the last of the attackers fled, a tense silence settled over the monastery. The team, bruised and exhausted, gathered in the central hall, their eyes fixed on the glowing relic.

Reed approached the altar, his heart pounding with relief and pride. "We did it. We protected the relic."

Emily, her face flushed with exertion, nodded. "The rituals held. The protective barriers are stronger than ever."

Gabriel, breathing heavily, added, "We fought them off. But we need to stay vigilant. They'll be back."

Graves, his expression serious, spoke quietly. "We need to be ready for anything. This was just the beginning."

As the team began to assess the damage and regroup, a sense of camaraderie and determination filled the air. They knew the battle was far from over, but their unity and resolve had carried them through the first major assault.

Reed turned to his companions, his voice filled with gratitude. "Thank you, all of you. We couldn't have done this without each other."

Emily smiled, her eyes reflecting the firelight. "We're in this together. We always have been."

Gabriel, ever the pragmatist, added, "We need to repair the defenses and prepare for the next attack. We can't let our guard down."

Graves, his voice steady, said, "I'll do whatever it takes to protect the relic. You have my word."

Reed nodded, his expression resolute. "We'll protect the relic, and we'll stop the cult. Together."

Over the next few days, the team worked tirelessly to repair the monastery's defenses and reinforce the protective barriers. They knew that the cult would not give up easily, and they needed to be prepared for anything.

Emily continued to lead the rituals, her voice filled with conviction as she chanted the ancient prayers. The symbols on the walls glowed brightly, a testament to the power and faith that protected the relic.

Gabriel and Graves focused on strengthening the physical defenses, setting traps and fortifying the entrances. Their combined strength and strategy ensured that the monastery was well-protected against any future assaults.

Reed spent hours poring over ancient texts and inscriptions, seeking any additional knowledge or insight that could help them in their mission. He knew that their fight was far from over, and he was determined to do everything in his power to protect the relic.

One evening, as they gathered around the fire, a sense of calm and unity settled over the group. They knew that their journey was far from over, but they felt a renewed sense of purpose and determination.

Gabriel spoke up, his voice filled with resolve. "We've come a long way, and we've faced incredible challenges. But we're stronger for it. We'll protect the relic, no matter what."

Emily nodded, her eyes shining with conviction. "We're a team. We'll face whatever comes together."

Graves, his expression serious but hopeful, added, "I've seen what true strength looks like. And I'm honored to be a part of this team."

Reed, his voice filled with gratitude, said, "We're in this together. And we'll see it through to the end."

They clinked their cups together, the sound echoing in the still night air. For a moment, they allowed themselves to feel a sense of peace, knowing that they had done everything in their power to protect the relic and prepare for the battle that was sure to come.

As they sat together, the weight of their mission pressing heavily on their shoulders, they knew that the road ahead would be difficult and dangerous. But they also knew that they were not alone. They had each other, and they had the strength and faith to see their mission through to the end.

And with that knowledge, they felt a sense of peace and resolve, ready to face whatever trials lay ahead, together.

11

Echoes of the Past

The dawn broke over the ancient monastery, casting long shadows across the rugged landscape. Inside, the air was filled with the hushed sounds of preparation and the occasional murmur of conversation. Dr. Jonathan Reed, Emily Carter, Gabriel Martinez, and Anton Graves had faced down one of their greatest challenges yet, but they knew their mission was far from over.

Reed sat at the large wooden table in the central hall, surrounded by ancient texts and manuscripts. The relic, now safely ensconced within its protective casing, lay nearby. Emily entered, carrying a tray of steaming tea.

"Thought you might need this," she said, setting the tray down.

"Thanks," Reed replied, gratefully accepting a cup. "We've got a lot of work ahead of us."

Emily nodded, taking a seat across from him. "What's our next move?"

"We need to find out more about the relic's origins and its significance," Reed said. "There's something we're missing—something that might give us the edge we need to protect it."

Gabriel entered the room, his expression serious. "I've reinforced the defenses, but we can't rely on them alone. We need a plan."

Reed looked thoughtful. "Graves mentioned the cult's connections. We need to find out who they're working with and cut off their resources."

Emily turned to Gabriel. "Do we have any contacts who might have information on the cult's operations?"

Gabriel nodded. "I've got a few people I can reach out to. It'll take some time, but it's worth a shot."

Graves appeared in the doorway, his face lined with concern. "I've been thinking about the attack. They knew exactly where to hit us. We have a leak—someone feeding them information."

Reed frowned. "Any idea who it might be?"

Graves shook his head. "Not yet. But we need to find out. Quickly."

Emily stood, her eyes blazing with determination. "Then let's get to work. We'll dig into the cult's connections, track down any leaks, and find out everything we can about the relic's history."

The days that followed were a blur of activity. Gabriel reached out to his contacts, gathering information on the cult's movements and resources. Emily and Reed pored over the ancient texts, seeking any clues that might shed light on the relic's origins. Graves, driven by a desire for redemption, worked tirelessly to uncover the identity of the leak.

One evening, as the sun set over the mountains, Gabriel returned from a meeting with one of his contacts. He found Reed and Emily in the library, surrounded by piles of books and scrolls.

"I've got news," Gabriel said, his voice low. "My contact confirmed that the cult is receiving significant funding from a shadowy figure known only as 'The Benefactor.' They've also been using a network of informants to track our movements."

Reed looked up, his eyes narrowing. "Did your contact have any information on who The Benefactor might be?"

Gabriel shook his head. "No, but he's digging deeper. We should have more information soon."

Emily leaned back in her chair, her brow furrowed in thought. "We need to cut off their funding and disrupt their network. If we can find out who The Benefactor is, we might be able to gain the upper hand."

Reed nodded. "Agreed. In the meantime, we need to focus on the relic. There's something here—something we're missing."

Late that night, Emily was alone in the library, a single candle flickering on the table before her. She was deep in a particularly old manuscript, her eyes straining to make out the faded text. Suddenly, a passage caught her attention.

"Jonathan," she called, her voice urgent. "I think I've found something."

Reed, who had been working in a nearby room, hurried over. "What is it?"

Emily pointed to the passage. "It's an account from one of the early guardians of the relic. He speaks of a hidden power—something that can only be unlocked by someone with a pure heart and unwavering faith."

Reed's eyes widened. "That could be the key. If we can unlock that power, we might be able to protect the relic more effectively."

Emily nodded. "But it's not clear how to do it. We need more information."

Reed's expression was determined. "Then we keep searching. We're close, Emily. I can feel it."

The following day, Graves approached Reed and Gabriel in the courtyard. His expression was grim. "I've found the leak."

Reed's eyes narrowed. "Who is it?"

Graves took a deep breath. "It's one of the monks from the monastery. He's been feeding information to the cult in exchange for money."

Gabriel's jaw tightened. "We need to confront him. Now."

Reed nodded. "Let's go."

They found the monk in a secluded part of the monastery, his demeanor nervous and guilty. Reed stepped forward, his voice cold. "We know what you've been doing."

The monk's eyes widened in fear. "I didn't have a choice! They threatened my family!"

Gabriel's voice was like steel. "And you chose to betray us instead? Do you realize what you've done?"

Tears streamed down the monk's face. "I'm sorry! I never wanted to hurt anyone. Please, forgive me."

Reed's expression softened slightly. "We need your help. If you truly want to make amends, tell us everything you know about the cult's plans."

The monk nodded, his voice trembling. "I'll tell you everything. Just please, protect my family."

With the monk's information, they learned that the cult was planning another attack, this time with even greater force. They had to act quickly to prepare. As they fortified their defenses and devised strategies, the pressure mounted. The fate of the relic—and perhaps the world—hung in the balance.

Reed gathered his team in the central hall, the tension palpable. "We know they're coming. We need to be ready for anything."

Gabriel's voice was firm. "We'll hold them off. We've done it before, and we can do it again."

Emily's eyes were fierce. "And this time, we have the advantage. We know their plans, and we're ready."

Graves, his expression resolute, added, "I'll do whatever it takes to protect the relic. We can't let them win."

Reed nodded, a sense of unity and determination filling the room. "Then let's prepare. We'll protect the relic, no matter the cost."

The night before the anticipated attack, Emily stood alone in the library, her thoughts heavy. She was startled by the sound of footsteps and turned to see Reed approaching.

"Can't sleep?" he asked, a gentle smile on his face.

Emily shook her head. "Too much on my mind. I keep thinking about what that manuscript said. About the hidden power of the relic."

Reed nodded, joining her at the table. "I've been thinking about that too. If we can unlock that power, it might be our best chance."

Emily's voice was quiet but determined. "I believe we can do it, Jonathan. We've come so far. We can't give up now."

Reed placed a hand on her shoulder, his touch reassuring. "We won't. We'll face this together."

As dawn broke, the monastery was eerily quiet, the calm before the storm. The team took their positions, their hearts heavy with anticipation. They knew the cult's forces would come, and they had to be ready.

The first signs of the attack came with a distant rumble, growing steadily louder. Gabriel, stationed at the main entrance, signaled to the others. "They're here."

Reed's voice was steady. "Everyone, hold your positions. Remember, our primary goal is to protect the relic."

The cultists appeared on the horizon, their numbers overwhelming. They advanced with a fanatical intensity, their eyes fixed on the monastery.

Gabriel braced himself. "Get ready!"

The battle began with a clash of steel and the shouts of combatants. Gabriel and Graves fought fiercely at the main entrance, their movements precise and controlled. Emily and Reed defended the secondary entrances, their determination unwavering.

As the cultists pressed forward, Emily's voice rang out with the ancient prayers and rituals, reinforcing the protective barriers around the relic. The symbols on the walls glowed brightly, responding to her invocations.

"We can't let them break through!" Reed shouted, deflecting a blow aimed at Emily.

Emily's eyes blazed with determination. "We won't. Keep fighting!"

Gabriel, holding his ground at the main entrance, called out to Graves. "How are you holding up?"

Graves, fighting with a newfound purpose, responded through gritted teeth. "We're managing, but they keep coming. We need to find a way to turn the tide."

Reed, overhearing the exchange, shouted back. "Emily, can you do it? Can you unlock the power of the relic?"

Emily's voice was filled with conviction. "I'll try. Cover me!"

Reed and Gabriel moved to hold off the attackers, giving Emily the space she needed. She approached the altar, her voice rising in a powerful chant. The air around her seemed to vibrate with energy, the symbols on the walls glowing even brighter.

The cultists hesitated, their movements faltering as the power of Emily's invocations took hold. The relic began to glow, its light growing stronger with each passing moment.

Gabriel fought with renewed vigor, his movements precise and controlled. "We can do this! Just a little longer!"

The leader of the cultists, a tall, imposing figure with a scarred face, advanced toward the central hall, his eyes fixed on the glowing relic. "You will not stop us!"

Reed's voice was firm. "We will protect the relic. No matter what."

Gabriel and Graves moved to intercept the cult leader, their combined strength and strategy overwhelming him. The remaining cultists, seeing their leader defeated, began to retreat, their fanatical resolve broken.

As the last of the attackers fled, a tense silence settled over the monastery. The team, bruised and exhausted, gathered in the central hall, their eyes fixed on the glowing relic.

Emily approached the altar, her heart pounding with relief and pride. "We did it. We unlocked the relic's power."

Reed's voice was filled with gratitude. "We protected the relic. Together."

Gabriel, breathing heavily, added, "But we need to stay vigilant. This isn't over."

Graves, his expression serious, spoke quietly. "We need to find out more about The Benefactor. They won't stop until they have the relic."

Reed nodded, a sense of unity and determination filling the room. "Then let's get to work. We'll protect the relic, and we'll stop the cult. Together."

Over the next few days, the team worked tirelessly to repair the monastery's defenses and reinforce the protective barriers. They knew that the cult would not give up easily, and they needed to be prepared for anything.

Emily continued to lead the rituals, her voice filled with conviction as she chanted the ancient prayers. The symbols on the walls glowed brightly, a testament to the power and faith that protected the relic.

Gabriel and Graves focused on strengthening the physical defenses, setting traps and fortifying the entrances. Their combined strength and strategy ensured that the monastery was well-protected against any future assaults.

Reed spent hours poring over ancient texts and inscriptions, seeking any additional knowledge or insight that could help them in their mission. He knew that their fight was far from over, and he was determined to do everything in his power to protect the relic.

One evening, as they gathered around the fire, a sense of calm and unity settled over the group. They knew that their journey was far from over, but they felt a renewed sense of purpose and determination.

Gabriel spoke up, his voice filled with resolve. "We've come a long way, and we've faced incredible challenges. But we're stronger for it. We'll protect the relic, no matter what."

Emily nodded, her eyes shining with conviction. "We're a team. We'll face whatever comes together."

Graves, his expression serious but hopeful, added, "I've seen what true strength looks like. And I'm honored to be a part of this team."

Reed, his voice filled with gratitude, said, "We're in this together. And we'll see it through to the end."

They clinked their cups together, the sound echoing in the still night air. For a moment, they allowed themselves to feel a sense of peace, knowing that they had done everything in their power to protect the relic and prepare for the battle that was sure to come.

As they sat together, the weight of their mission pressing heavily on their shoulders, they knew that the road ahead would be difficult and dangerous. But they also knew that they were not alone. They had each other, and they had the strength and faith to see their mission through to the end.

And with that knowledge, they felt a sense of peace and resolve, ready to face whatever trials lay ahead, together.

12

A New Alliance

The atmosphere inside the ancient monastery was a mix of determined energy and cautious optimism. The team had weathered another attack, but they knew the cult wouldn't give up easily. Dr. Jonathan Reed, Emily Carter, Gabriel Martinez, and Anton Graves gathered around the large wooden table in the central hall, where the relic rested securely.

"We've done well so far," Reed began, looking around at his team. "But we can't let our guard down. We need to take proactive steps to find The Benefactor and cut off the cult's resources."

Gabriel nodded. "I've reached out to some of my contacts. They're gathering intel on possible leads. It'll take some time, but we should have something concrete soon."

Emily's eyes sparkled with determination. "Meanwhile, we should continue strengthening the monastery's defenses and delve deeper into the relic's history. There might be more we can learn to help us."

Graves leaned forward, his expression serious. "We also need to think about alliances. There are other groups out there who oppose the cult. If we can bring them to our side, we'll have a better chance of stopping The Benefactor."

Reed considered this, nodding slowly. "Good point, Graves. We can't do this alone. Let's start reaching out to potential allies. Gabriel, you handle the contacts. Emily and I will continue our research."

Over the next few days, the team worked tirelessly. Gabriel's contacts began to send in snippets of information, giving them leads on The Benefactor's possible identity and operations. Meanwhile, Emily and Reed continued to pour over ancient texts and manuscripts, seeking any clues that might help them unlock more of the relic's power.

One afternoon, Gabriel burst into the library, a triumphant grin on his face. "We've got a lead. My contact in Istanbul identified a high-ranking member of the cult who might know The Benefactor's identity. He's willing to meet with us."

Reed looked up from a dusty tome, his eyes gleaming with interest. "That's fantastic news. When can we meet him?"

"Tomorrow," Gabriel replied. "We'll need to leave tonight to make it in time."

Emily closed her book, excitement and determination evident on her face. "I'll get our things ready. We need to be prepared for anything."

Graves, who had been listening quietly, spoke up. "We should be cautious. It could be a trap."

Reed nodded. "Agreed. We'll proceed carefully. But this could be the break we've been waiting for."

The journey to Istanbul was swift but tense. They traveled under the cover of darkness, moving through the bustling city with purpose. Their contact had arranged a meeting at a secluded café in a less frequented part of town.

As they entered the café, Reed, Emily, Gabriel, and Graves scanned the room, their senses heightened. A man in his late forties, with sharp features and a wary expression, sat at a corner table. He looked up as they approached, his eyes flicking to each of them in turn.

"Mr. Ali?" Gabriel asked, his voice low and cautious.

The man nodded. "Yes. You must be Gabriel. Please, sit."

They took their seats, the atmosphere tense but cordial. Ali leaned forward, his voice barely above a whisper. "I don't have much time. The cult is everywhere. What do you want to know?"

Reed spoke first. "We need information on The Benefactor. Who is he, and where can we find him?"

Ali glanced around nervously before responding. "The Benefactor is a very powerful and secretive figure. Few within the cult know his true identity. But there are rumors. One name keeps coming up—Leonid Markov, a wealthy industrialist with ties to various underground networks."

Emily leaned in, her expression intense. "Do you know where we can find him?"

Ali hesitated. "He's a difficult man to reach. He operates out of several locations, always on the move. But I've heard whispers about a private estate on the outskirts of Vienna. It's heavily guarded, but if you can get in, you might find what you're looking for."

Gabriel nodded. "Thank you, Ali. You've been a great help."

Ali glanced around once more, his anxiety palpable. "Be careful. The cult doesn't take kindly to betrayal. And Markov is more dangerous than you can imagine."

Reed stood, offering his hand. "We appreciate the warning. We'll be careful."

Ali shook his hand, then slipped out of the café, disappearing into the bustling streets of Istanbul. The team exchanged looks, the gravity of their mission settling over them.

"Vienna, then," Emily said, her voice firm. "We need to move quickly."

Gabriel nodded. "I'll make the arrangements. We leave tonight."

The flight to Vienna was filled with tense anticipation. Upon arrival, they made their way to a small, nondescript safehouse where they could plan their next move. Gabriel spread a detailed map of Markov's estate on the table, pointing out key locations and potential entry points.

"The estate is heavily guarded," Gabriel explained. "We'll need to be smart about this. Stealth is our best option."

Emily nodded. "We should gather as much information as we can before making our move. Surveillance, local contacts—anything that might give us an edge."

Graves, studying the map intently, added, "We need to identify the best entry points and potential escape routes. If things go south, we need to be ready to get out quickly."

Reed looked around at his team, feeling a mix of pride and determination. "This is it. We've come a long way, and we've faced incredible challenges. But we're ready for this. Let's get to work."

Over the next two days, the team conducted thorough surveillance of Markov's estate. They observed the guards' patterns, the layout of the buildings, and any potential weak points. Gabriel used his contacts to gather additional intel, while Emily and Reed continued to research any historical connections that might help them understand Markov's interest in the relic.

One evening, as they gathered in the safehouse to discuss their findings, Gabriel laid out their plan. "We'll go in under the cover of darkness. There's a service entrance on the west side that's less guarded. Once inside, we split up. Emily and Reed, you head for Markov's study—there's a good chance that's where he keeps any sensitive information. Graves and I will create a diversion and handle any guards we encounter."

Emily's eyes were sharp with determination. "What do we do if we find Markov?"

Gabriel's expression was grim. "We get the information we need, whatever it takes. But remember, the primary objective is to identify and locate The Benefactor."

Reed nodded. "We've got this. Let's be careful and stay focused."

Under the cover of darkness, they approached Markov's estate. The air was cool and still, the only sounds those of their careful footsteps and the distant hum of the city. They reached the service entrance without incident, slipping inside and moving quietly through the dimly lit corridors.

"Remember, stay close and stay quiet," Gabriel whispered. "We need to move quickly."

Emily and Reed headed towards the main building, their senses heightened. The corridors were lined with ornate tapestries and antique furnishings, a stark contrast to the tension in the air. They reached the door to Markov's study, finding it locked.

"Stand back," Emily whispered, pulling out a set of lock-picking tools. Within moments, she had the door open, and they slipped inside.

The study was lavishly decorated, with shelves of books and a large, imposing desk. Emily began searching through the papers on the desk while Reed scanned the room for anything unusual.

"Over here," Emily whispered, holding up a document. "It's a letter from Markov to someone named 'L.' It mentions the relic and plans for an upcoming operation."

Reed's eyes narrowed. "L could be The Benefactor. We need to find out more."

Suddenly, they heard footsteps approaching the study. "Hide!" Reed hissed, pulling Emily behind a large bookcase.

The door opened, and a tall, imposing man entered. He moved to the desk, sifting through the papers with a look of frustration. Reed recognized him from the description they had received—this was Markov.

"We need that relic," Markov muttered to himself. "L won't wait forever. We need to secure it and deliver it to him before it's too late."

Emily's eyes widened, and she exchanged a look with Reed. This was the confirmation they needed. Markov was indeed working for The Benefactor.

As Markov turned to leave, Emily's hand slipped, knocking a book off the shelf. Markov spun around, his eyes narrowing. "Who's there?"

Reed acted quickly, stepping out from behind the bookcase. "Looking for something, Markov?"

Markov's eyes flashed with anger and surprise. "You! How did you get in here?"

Reed stepped forward, his expression cold. "That's not important. What matters is that we know you're working for The Benefactor. Tell us everything you know, and maybe we'll let you walk out of here."

Markov sneered. "You think you can intimidate me? You have no idea what you're up against."

Emily stepped out from behind the bookcase, her eyes fierce. "We know enough. Now talk."

Markov's expression hardened, but before he could respond, the sound of a struggle echoed from the corridor. Gabriel and Graves burst into the room, followed by two guards who were quickly subdued.

"We need to move," Gabriel said urgently. "More guards are on their way."

Reed turned to Markov. "You're coming with us."

Markov glared at him but didn't resist. They moved quickly through the corridors, making their way to the service entrance. As they emerged into the night, the sound of approaching footsteps grew louder.

"This way!" Graves shouted, leading them to a waiting vehicle.

They piled in, and Gabriel gunned the engine, speeding away from the estate. As they put distance between themselves and Markov's guards, Reed turned to their captive.

"Now, Markov," he said, his voice cold. "Tell us everything you know about The Benefactor."

Back at the safehouse, Markov was securely restrained in a chair, his expression a mix of anger and defiance. Reed, Emily, Gabriel, and Graves stood before him, their eyes fixed on him with unwavering determination.

"You can't get away with this," Markov spat. "The Benefactor will find you. He'll destroy you."

Reed's voice was icy. "We'll take our chances. Now talk. Who is The Benefactor, and where can we find him?"

Markov hesitated, then finally spoke. "You don't understand. The Benefactor is more powerful than you can imagine. He has connections everywhere—politicians, military, the underworld. You're fighting a losing battle."

Emily's eyes blazed. "We're not giving up. Tell us where to find him."

Markov's shoulders slumped. "Fine. There's a private island off the coast of Greece. That's where he's been hiding. But you'll never get close. The place is a fortress."

Gabriel's eyes narrowed. "We'll see about that. What else can you tell us?"

Markov sighed. "He's obsessed with the relic. He believes it holds the key to ultimate power. If he gets his hands on it, there's no telling what he'll do."

Reed exchanged a look with Emily and Gabriel. "Then we need to get to him first. We'll need to plan carefully, but we can do this."

Graves, his expression resolute, added, "We're running out of time. We need to move quickly."

The next few days were spent meticulously planning their assault on The Benefactor's island fortress. Gabriel used his contacts to gather as much information as possible about the island's defenses and layout. Emily and Reed continued their research, seeking any advantage they could find.

As they prepared for the mission, a sense of unity and determination filled the air. They knew the stakes were higher than ever, but they were ready to face whatever challenges lay ahead.

One evening, as they gathered in the safehouse, Reed spoke up. "We've come a long way, and we've faced incredible challenges. But we're ready for this. We'll stop The Benefactor and protect the relic."

Emily nodded, her eyes shining with conviction. "We're a team. We'll face whatever comes together."

Gabriel raised his glass in a toast. "To the mission. And to protecting the legacy we've been entrusted with."

Graves, his expression serious but hopeful, added, "To redemption. And to doing what's right."

They clinked their glasses together, the sound echoing in the still night air. For a moment, they allowed themselves to feel a sense of peace, knowing that they had done everything in their power to prepare for the battle that was sure to come.

As they sat together, the weight of their mission pressing heavily on their shoulders, they knew that the road ahead would be difficult and dangerous. But they also knew that they were not alone. They had each other, and they had the strength and faith to see their mission through to the end.

And with that knowledge, they felt a sense of peace and resolve, ready to face whatever trials lay ahead, together.

13

The Assault on the Fortress

The quiet of the early morning was punctuated by the hum of the engine as the team made their way toward the coast. Dr. Jonathan Reed, Emily Carter, Gabriel Martinez, and Anton Graves were focused and determined, each of them aware of the gravity of their mission. They had spent days meticulously planning their assault on The Benefactor's island fortress, and now, as they neared their destination, the reality of what lay ahead began to set in.

Reed sat in the front seat, his eyes scanning the horizon. "We're getting close," he said, turning to the rest of the team. "Everyone ready?"

Gabriel nodded from the driver's seat. "As ready as we'll ever be. The boat's waiting for us just up ahead."

Emily, sitting beside Graves in the back, took a deep breath. "This is it. We've come so far. We can't let anything stop us now."

Graves, his expression resolute, added, "We won't. We're going to end this."

They reached the small dock where a sleek, black speedboat was moored. Gabriel killed the engine, and they quickly unloaded their gear, moving with practiced efficiency. As they boarded the boat, Gabriel briefed them one last time.

"The island is heavily fortified. We'll approach from the south side, where the defenses are weakest. Once we're ashore, we split into two teams. Reed and Emily, you head for The Benefactor's main quarters. Graves and I will handle the guards and create a diversion."

Reed nodded, tightening the strap on his backpack. "Let's move quickly and stay focused. We've got one shot at this."

Emily gave a determined nod. "We'll make it count."

The boat cut through the waves, the roar of the engine lost in the wind. As they neared the island, the imposing silhouette of The Benefactor's fortress loomed larger, its high walls and watchtowers casting long shadows over the water.

Gabriel guided the boat into a small cove, hidden from the main defenses. They anchored and slipped into the water, swimming silently to the shore. The cold water bit at their skin, but they pressed on, driven by the urgency of their mission.

Reed was the first to reach the shore, pulling himself onto the rocky beach and helping the others out of the water. They quickly moved to the cover of the trees, their wet clothes clinging to them as they caught their breath.

"Alright," Gabriel whispered, pulling out a map. "From here, we head up this path. It'll take us to the outer wall. There's a drainage tunnel that should get us inside."

Emily peered into the dense underbrush. "Let's move. We don't have much time."

They made their way through the trees, moving quickly and quietly. The path was narrow and overgrown, but they navigated it with ease, their senses heightened by the anticipation of what lay ahead.

As they reached the outer wall, Gabriel pointed to a rusted grate partially hidden by vines. "This is it. I'll get it open."

Graves and Reed kept watch while Gabriel worked on the grate. Within moments, he had it open, and they slipped inside the drainage tunnel, the sound of dripping water echoing around them.

The tunnel was dark and narrow, the air damp and musty. They moved single file, their flashlights casting eerie shadows on the walls. After several minutes, the tunnel widened into a larger chamber, and they could see a faint light filtering through a grate above.

Gabriel climbed up, peering through the grate. "Looks clear. Let's go."

They climbed out of the tunnel, finding themselves in a small courtyard within the fortress walls. The sound of distant voices and the clink of armor echoed through the air, but the courtyard itself was empty.

Reed glanced around, his mind racing. "This way. The main quarters should be just beyond that archway."

Gabriel nodded. "Remember, we split up here. Reed, Emily—good luck."

"Stay safe," Emily replied, giving them a determined look. "We'll see you soon."

Reed and Emily moved quickly through the archway, their footsteps silent on the stone path. The fortress was a labyrinth of corridors and chambers, but they navigated it with the confidence born of careful planning and preparation.

As they approached the central building, the sense of anticipation grew. They knew The Benefactor was inside, and they had to be ready for anything.

"Stay close," Reed whispered, his eyes scanning their surroundings. "We don't know what we're walking into."

Emily nodded, her expression fierce. "We're ready. Let's do this."

They slipped into the main building, the air cool and heavy with the scent of old stone and burning candles. The corridors were dimly lit, the flickering light casting eerie shadows on the walls.

Reed led the way, his senses heightened. They moved silently, their footsteps barely making a sound. As they turned a corner, they heard voices coming from a nearby room.

"That must be it," Reed whispered, gesturing to a heavy wooden door. "Ready?"

Emily nodded, gripping her weapon tightly. "Ready."

Reed pushed the door open, and they slipped inside, their eyes scanning the room. It was a large, opulent chamber, filled with antique furniture and lavish decorations. At the far end of the room, a man stood with his back to them, staring out of a large window.

"The Benefactor," Emily whispered, her eyes narrowing.

Reed stepped forward, his voice cold. "Markov, or should I say The Benefactor?"

The man turned slowly, a cold smile on his lips. "Dr. Reed, Ms. Carter. I've been expecting you."

Emily's eyes blazed with anger. "It's over, Markov. We know everything. Surrender now, and this doesn't have to end badly."

Markov's smile widened. "You're bold, I'll give you that. But you have no idea what you're up against."

Reed's voice was steady. "We know enough. We know about your plans for the relic, and we're here to stop you."

Markov's eyes flickered with amusement. "Stop me? You're too late. The ritual is already in motion. Soon, the relic's power will be mine."

Emily stepped forward, her voice filled with determination. "We won't let that happen."

Markov's expression hardened. "Then you leave me no choice."

He raised his hand, and the air around him seemed to shimmer with energy. Reed and Emily braced themselves, ready for a fight.

Meanwhile, Gabriel and Graves were making their way through the fortress, dealing with the guards and creating distractions to keep the cult's forces occupied. They moved with precision and efficiency, their movements coordinated and deliberate.

Gabriel glanced at Graves as they rounded a corner. "We need to keep the pressure on. Reed and Emily need time to deal with Markov."

Graves nodded, his expression grim. "Let's give them everything we've got."

They continued their assault, taking out guards and setting traps to slow down the cult's forces. The sound of gunfire and shouts echoed through the corridors, the fortress a battleground.

Back in the opulent chamber, the fight had begun in earnest. Markov's power crackled in the air, the energy swirling around him as he launched his attacks. Reed and Emily moved with agility and precision, dodging his attacks and countering with their own.

"We need to break his concentration!" Reed shouted, deflecting a bolt of energy.

Emily nodded, her eyes sharp. "I'll distract him. You go for the relic."

She launched herself at Markov, her movements swift and controlled. Markov's eyes widened in surprise as Emily's attack forced him to focus on her, giving Reed the opening he needed.

Reed moved quickly, reaching the altar where the relic was placed. He grabbed it, feeling the warmth of its power surge through him.

"Emily, I've got it!" he shouted, turning back to her.

Emily dodged another attack, her eyes blazing with determination. "Good! Now let's end this!"

Reed focused on the relic, tapping into its power. The symbols on the walls glowed brightly, responding to his invocation. The air around them vibrated with energy, and Markov's attacks began to falter.

"No!" Markov shouted, his voice filled with desperation. "You can't do this!"

Emily moved in, her movements swift and precise. She struck Markov, her attack fueled by the power of the relic. Markov cried out, his defenses crumbling.

Reed joined her, the two of them working in perfect harmony. Together, they channeled the relic's power, their combined strength overwhelming Markov.

With a final, desperate cry, Markov fell to the ground, the energy around him dissipating. The chamber fell silent, the air heavy with the aftermath of the battle.

Gabriel and Graves burst into the room, their expressions tense. "Is it over?" Gabriel asked, his eyes scanning the scene.

Reed nodded, his breath coming in heavy gasps. "It's over. Markov is defeated."

Emily's expression was one of relief and determination. "We did it. The relic is safe."

Graves approached Markov, his expression cold. "What do we do with him?"

Reed's voice was firm. "We take him back with us. He has a lot to answer for."

Gabriel nodded. "Agreed. Let's get out of here before reinforcements arrive."

They moved quickly, securing Markov and making their way back through the fortress. The cult's forces had been thrown into disarray by their attack, and they encountered little resistance as they made their escape.

As they reached the boat, the first light of dawn began to break over the horizon. They boarded quickly, Gabriel taking the helm and guiding them away from the island.

Reed sat beside Emily, the relic safely in his hands. "We did it," he said, his voice filled with a mix of exhaustion and relief.

Emily nodded, her eyes shining with determination. "We stopped him. But we need to stay vigilant. There are others out there who will try to take the relic."

Gabriel, steering the boat, added, "We'll face whatever comes next. Together."

Graves, his expression serious but hopeful, said, "We've come this far. We can handle anything."

As the boat sped away from the island, the team felt a sense of unity and determination. They had faced incredible challenges and emerged victorious, but they knew their mission was far from over.

Together, they would protect the relic and the legacy of those who had come before them. And they would be ready to face whatever trials lay ahead, united by their shared purpose and unwavering faith.

And with that knowledge, they felt a sense of peace and resolve, ready to face whatever the future held, together.

14

The Final Revelation

The return journey from the island fortress was tense but victorious. Dr. Jonathan Reed, Emily Carter, Gabriel Martinez, and Anton Graves had managed to defeat Markov and secure the relic. The early morning light painted the sky in hues of pink and gold as they sped across the water, leaving the island and its secrets behind.

Reed sat at the helm, guiding the boat through the gentle waves. The relic was safely tucked away in a secure compartment, its power now under their protection. Emily, Gabriel, and Graves sat quietly, each lost in their thoughts as they processed the events of the past few days.

"We did it," Emily finally said, breaking the silence. "We stopped Markov."

Gabriel nodded, his expression serious. "We did, but we can't let our guard down. The Benefactor's network is still out there. We need to find out who else might be after the relic."

Reed glanced back at Graves, who was watching the horizon with a pensive look. "Graves, you've been invaluable to us. Do you have any idea who else might be connected to The Benefactor?"

Graves shook his head slowly. "Markov was the highest-ranking member I knew. But the cult is vast. There could be others with the same level of power and influence. We need to stay vigilant."

They reached the mainland by midday, docking the boat at a small, secluded marina. Gabriel had arranged for transportation, and within the hour, they were on their way to a safe house in the countryside. The drive was long and uneventful, the quiet countryside a stark contrast to the chaos they had left behind.

The safe house was a small, rustic cabin nestled in a dense forest. It was well-hidden and secure, the perfect place to regroup and plan their next move. As they settled in, Reed gathered the team around the large wooden table in the living room.

"We need to figure out our next steps," he said, his voice steady. "Markov may be defeated, but we can't assume the threat is over. We need to stay ahead of any potential threats."

Emily nodded. "Agreed. We should continue researching the relic's history and any potential connections to other powerful figures. There might be clues we've overlooked."

Gabriel added, "And we need to strengthen our defenses. The relic's power is too great to risk losing it again."

Graves leaned forward, his expression resolute. "I'll keep digging into the cult's network. There might be someone we missed—someone who can give us more information on The Benefactor's plans."

Reed looked around at his team, feeling a surge of pride and determination. "Then let's get to work. We've come this far, and we can't stop now."

Over the next few days, the team settled into a routine. Reed and Emily spent hours pouring over ancient texts and manuscripts, seeking any clues that might help them understand the relic's true power and purpose. Gabriel focused on reinforcing the safe house's defenses, setting traps and securing the perimeter. Graves continued his investigation into the cult's network, using his connections to gather any information he could find.

One evening, as they gathered around the table for dinner, Emily shared a discovery she had made. "I found a reference to a hidden sanctuary—another one, like the ones we've already found. It's located deep in the mountains, and it was built to protect powerful artifacts, much like our relic."

Reed's eyes lit up with interest. "Do you think it could hold more information about the relic's origins?"

Emily nodded. "It's possible. The texts mentioned that the sanctuary was designed to be a place of last resort, where the most important artifacts and knowledge were kept safe."

Gabriel leaned forward. "Then we need to find it. It could be the key to understanding the relic and protecting it from any future threats."

Graves added, "And it might give us more insight into The Benefactor's plans. If we can find out what he's after, we can stay one step ahead."

Reed looked around at his team, feeling a renewed sense of purpose. "Then it's settled. We'll find this sanctuary and uncover its secrets. It's our best chance at protecting the relic and stopping The Benefactor once and for all."

The journey to the hidden sanctuary was long and arduous. They traveled by car as far as the roads would take them, then continued on foot through rugged mountain terrain. The air grew colder as they ascended, the landscape becoming more remote and desolate with each step.

"We're close," Emily said, consulting her map. "The entrance should be just up ahead."

They reached a narrow path that led to a steep, rocky cliff face. The entrance to the sanctuary was hidden behind a dense thicket of trees and underbrush. Gabriel pushed through the foliage, revealing a small, narrow cave entrance.

"This is it," he said, his voice echoing in the confined space. "Let's go."

They entered the cave, moving carefully through the narrow passage. The air was cool and damp, the walls lined with ancient carvings and symbols. As they ventured deeper, the passage widened into a large chamber, the ceiling high above them.

"This place is incredible," Emily whispered, her voice filled with awe. "It's like walking through history."

Reed nodded, his eyes scanning the chamber. "Let's find out what secrets it holds."

They spread out, exploring the chamber and examining the carvings on the walls. Emily found a series of inscriptions that detailed the sanctuary's purpose and the artifacts it was designed to protect.

"These inscriptions mention a powerful artifact," Emily said, her eyes wide with excitement. "It was hidden here to protect it from those who would misuse its power."

Gabriel joined her, studying the carvings. "Do they mention what the artifact is?"

Emily nodded. "Yes, it describes a relic of immense power, capable of great good or great harm, depending on who wields it."

Reed's mind raced. "This sounds like our relic. There must be more information here—something that can help us understand its true purpose."

As they continued their search, Graves found a hidden compartment in the wall. He pried it open, revealing a small, ancient chest. Inside, they found a collection of scrolls and a beautifully crafted, ornate key.

"This key must open something important," Graves said, holding it up. "Maybe it leads to the artifact."

Emily examined the key, her eyes lighting up. "Look at the symbols—it matches the carvings on the wall. There must be a hidden chamber somewhere in this sanctuary."

Reed nodded. "Let's find it. This could be the breakthrough we've been looking for."

They searched the chamber, looking for any sign of a hidden door or passage. After several minutes, Gabriel found a section of the wall that felt different—a faint outline of a door hidden beneath layers of dust and grime.

"Here," Gabriel said, pointing to the outline. "This has to be it."

Reed inserted the key into a small, barely visible keyhole. With a soft click, the wall shifted, revealing a narrow passage leading to a hidden chamber.

They entered the chamber, their flashlights illuminating the ancient stone walls. The air was thick with the scent of age and history, and the symbols on the walls glowed faintly in the light.

In the center of the chamber stood a pedestal, upon which rested a small, intricately carved box. Emily approached it carefully, her heart pounding with anticipation.

"This must be it," she whispered, opening the box. Inside, they found a collection of ancient scrolls, each one carefully preserved.

Reed picked up one of the scrolls, unrolling it carefully. "These scrolls could contain the answers we've been looking for."

As they examined the scrolls, Emily found one that detailed the history of the relic and its true purpose. "Listen to this," she said, her voice filled with excitement. "The relic was created by an ancient order, designed to protect and guide those who possessed it. But it also warned of the dangers of misusing its power."

Gabriel leaned in, his eyes wide. "What kind of dangers?"

Emily continued reading. "The scrolls mention a prophecy—one that speaks of a great conflict, where the relic's power would be the deciding factor. It also mentions a 'chosen one,' someone with the strength and purity of heart to wield the relic's power for good."

Reed's mind raced. "This prophecy—it sounds like it could be coming true. We need to make sure the relic is used for the right purpose."

Graves added, "And we need to find out who the 'chosen one' is. If we can identify them, we can protect them and ensure the relic's power is used for good."

As they absorbed the information from the scrolls, a sense of urgency and determination filled the air. They knew they had uncovered something of immense importance—something that could change the course of their mission and the fate of the relic.

"We need to take these scrolls back with us," Reed said, carefully placing them in a secure container. "They could be the key to understanding the relic's true power."

Emily nodded. "And we need to continue our research. There might be more clues hidden in these texts—something that can help us identify the 'chosen one' and protect the relic."

Gabriel added, "And we need to stay vigilant. The Benefactor won't stop until he gets what he wants. We need to be ready for anything."

Graves, his expression resolute, said, "We've come this far. We can't give up now. We'll protect the relic and stop The Benefactor, no matter what."

The journey back to the safe house was filled with a renewed sense of purpose and determination. They knew they had uncovered something of immense importance, and they were ready to face whatever challenges lay ahead.

As they settled back into the safe house, Reed gathered the team around the table, the ancient scrolls spread out before them. "We've made an incredible discovery. These scrolls could be the key to understanding the relic's true purpose and stopping The Benefactor."

Emily nodded, her eyes shining with determination. "We need to keep digging, keep searching for answers. We're so close."

Gabriel added, "And we need to stay on guard. The Benefactor won't stop until he gets what he wants. We need to be ready for anything."

Graves, his expression serious but hopeful, said, "We've come this far. We can handle anything."

Reed looked around at his team, feeling a sense of pride and unity. "Then let's get to work. We've got a lot to do, but I know we can do it. Together."

As they continued their research, the weight of their mission pressed heavily on their shoulders. But they knew they were not alone. They had each other, and they had the strength and faith to see their mission through to the end.

And with that knowledge, they felt a sense of peace and resolve, ready to face whatever trials lay ahead, together.

15

The Chosen One

The sun cast a golden glow over the secluded safe house as Dr. Jonathan Reed, Emily Carter, Gabriel Martinez, and Anton Graves gathered in the living room, the ancient scrolls spread out before them. The atmosphere was thick with anticipation and urgency, as they delved into the texts, searching for clues about the relic's true purpose and the prophecy of the chosen one.

Reed traced his finger over the delicate parchment, his brow furrowed in concentration. "These scrolls mention a prophecy—a great conflict where the relic's power will be the deciding factor. It also speaks of a chosen one, someone with the strength and purity of heart to wield the relic for good."

Emily leaned over, her eyes scanning the text. "The chosen one... we need to figure out who that is. It could be the key to stopping The Benefactor and protecting the relic."

Gabriel, pacing the room, added, "And we need to do it fast. The Benefactor won't stop until he gets his hands on the relic."

Graves, his voice steady, said, "We need to find this chosen one before he does. If the prophecy is true, they're our best hope."

The days that followed were a whirlwind of research and planning. Emily and Reed spent hours poring over the ancient texts, seeking any clues that might help them identify the chosen one. Gabriel used his network of contacts to gather intelligence on The Benefactor's movements, while Graves continued to investigate the cult's network.

One afternoon, Emily discovered a passage that caught her attention. "Jonathan, look at this. It mentions a specific lineage—a bloodline that has been protected and hidden for generations. The chosen one is said to come from this line."

Reed's eyes lit up with interest. "If we can trace this lineage, we might be able to find the chosen one."

Emily nodded. "It's a long shot, but it's our best lead."

Gabriel, listening from across the room, approached them. "Do we have any idea where to start?"

Emily pointed to a map. "The scrolls mention a village in Eastern Europe, a place where the bloodline was last known to reside. It's remote and isolated—perfect for keeping something hidden."

Graves added, "We need to get there quickly. If The Benefactor catches wind of this, he'll be on our heels."

Reed agreed. "Then let's not waste any time. We leave at first light."

The journey to the village was long and challenging. They traveled by plane, train, and finally by car, navigating narrow, winding roads through dense forests and rugged terrain. The air grew colder as they ascended into the mountains, the landscape becoming more remote and desolate.

"We're getting close," Emily said, consulting her map. "The village should be just up ahead."

As they rounded a bend, the village came into view—a cluster of quaint, stone houses nestled in a valley, surrounded by towering peaks. The sight was almost idyllic, but the team knew the gravity of their mission.

They parked the car at the edge of the village and approached a small inn, the only establishment that seemed open. The innkeeper, a middle-aged woman with kind eyes, greeted them warmly.

"Welcome," she said, her voice carrying a faint accent. "What brings you to our village?"

Reed stepped forward, choosing his words carefully. "We're researchers, interested in the history of this area. We've heard there might be some old families here with deep roots."

The innkeeper's eyes narrowed slightly, but she nodded. "There are indeed old families here, with histories that go back centuries. If you're looking for information, you might want to speak with the village elder. He knows more about our history than anyone."

Emily smiled. "Thank you. Could you point us in his direction?"

The innkeeper gestured to a small house at the far end of the village. "He lives there. His name is Stefan. He's a bit of a recluse, but if you explain your purpose, he might be willing to help."

They made their way to Stefan's house, the villagers watching them with a mix of curiosity and wariness. The house was modest, with a well-tended garden and an air of quiet solitude. Reed knocked on the door, and after a moment, an elderly man answered. His eyes were sharp and intelligent, despite his age.

"Can I help you?" he asked, his tone cautious.

Reed introduced himself and his team, explaining their interest in the village's history and the lineage mentioned in the ancient texts. Stefan listened intently, his expression thoughtful.

"You've come a long way," he said finally. "And you're not the first to ask about this lineage. But I sense your intentions are different."

Emily stepped forward. "We're trying to protect something very important. We believe the chosen one mentioned in the prophecy is connected to this village."

Stefan's eyes narrowed. "Come inside. We have much to discuss."

Inside, Stefan led them to a cozy living room, where a fire crackled in the hearth. They sat down, and Stefan began to speak.

"The lineage you're seeking is indeed tied to this village," he said. "It goes back many generations, to a time when our ancestors fled persecution and sought refuge here. They carried with them a great secret, one that has been guarded and passed down through the ages."

Reed leaned forward. "Do you know where we can find the current descendant of this lineage?"

Stefan nodded. "Yes. Her name is Anya. She's a healer, living on the outskirts of the village. She's been told of her heritage but knows little of its significance. I'll take you to her."

They followed Stefan to a small cottage on the edge of the village. The garden was filled with medicinal herbs and flowers, and a sense of calm pervaded the air. Anya was outside, tending to her plants. She was in her late twenties, with an air of quiet strength and kindness.

"Anya," Stefan called gently. "These people have come to speak with you. It's important."

Anya stood up, brushing dirt from her hands. "Stefan, what's this about?"

Reed stepped forward. "Anya, we believe you are the descendant of a very important lineage. We're here to protect you and to help you understand your heritage."

Anya's eyes widened in surprise and confusion. "I've been told stories, but I never imagined they were true. What do you need from me?"

Emily approached her, her voice gentle. "We need your help to protect a powerful relic. There's a prophecy that speaks of a chosen one—someone from your lineage—who can wield its power for good."

Anya looked around at the team, her expression a mix of fear and determination. "I don't know if I'm this chosen one, but if what you say is true, I'll do whatever I can to help."

Graves, his voice steady, added, "We'll protect you, Anya. We're in this together."

Over the next few days, Anya was integrated into their team. They explained the significance of the relic, the prophecy, and the danger posed by The Benefactor. Anya proved to be a quick learner, her natural intuition and healing abilities hinting at a deeper connection to the relic.

One evening, as they gathered in Stefan's living room, Anya spoke up. "I've been thinking about the prophecy. If I'm truly meant to wield this relic, I need to understand its power. We need to perform the rituals and unlock its full potential."

Reed nodded. "Agreed. We need to find a safe place to perform the rituals, where we won't be interrupted."

Stefan suggested a nearby cave, known to the villagers as a place of spiritual significance. "It's secluded and has been used for sacred ceremonies for centuries. It's the perfect place for what you need to do."

Gabriel looked around at the team. "Then let's get ready. We'll head to the cave at first light."

The next morning, they made their way to the cave, carrying the relic and the necessary materials for the rituals. The air was crisp and cold, the forest quiet and serene. As they entered the cave, a sense of ancient power and sacredness filled the air.

Emily and Reed set up the altar, placing the relic at its center. Anya stood before it, her eyes closed, taking deep breaths to steady herself. The team formed a protective circle around her, their expressions focused and determined.

"Are you ready, Anya?" Reed asked, his voice gentle.

Anya opened her eyes, her expression resolute. "I'm ready."

Emily began the ritual, chanting the ancient prayers and invocations. The symbols on the walls began to glow faintly, responding to her words. Anya joined in, her voice strong and clear, as she called upon the power of her ancestors.

The air around them vibrated with energy, the relic glowing brighter with each passing moment. Anya reached out, her hands trembling, and placed them on the relic. A surge of power flowed through her, the light intensifying until it filled the entire cave.

Reed watched in awe as Anya's expression transformed, a look of understanding and clarity in her eyes. "I can feel it," she whispered. "The power... it's overwhelming, but I understand now. The relic's purpose is to protect and heal, to guide and strengthen those who wield it for good."

Gabriel, his voice filled with admiration, said, "You are the chosen one, Anya. You were meant for this."

Graves added, "And we'll stand by you, every step of the way."

As the ritual reached its climax, the light began to fade, the energy settling into a calm, steady glow. Anya lowered her hands, her expression serene and determined.

"We did it," she said softly. "The relic's power is fully unlocked."

Reed approached her, his eyes filled with respect. "You did it, Anya. You're ready."

Emily, her voice gentle, added, "Now we need to protect you and the relic from The Benefactor. We can't let him get his hands on this power."

Anya nodded. "I understand. I'm ready to fight, to protect this relic and fulfill my destiny."

As they left the cave, a sense of unity and purpose filled the air. They knew the battle was far from over, but with Anya by their side, they felt a renewed sense of hope and determination.

Back at the safe house, they continued their preparations, strengthening their defenses and planning their next move. They knew The Benefactor would not give up easily, and they had to be ready for anything.

One evening, as they gathered around the table, Reed spoke up. "We've made incredible progress, but we can't let our guard down. The Benefactor will come for us, and we need to be ready."

Gabriel nodded. "We'll stay vigilant. We've come too far to lose now."

Emily added, "And we have Anya. Together, we're stronger than ever."

Graves, his expression serious but hopeful, said, "We'll protect the relic and stop The Benefactor, no matter what."

Anya, her eyes filled with determination, added, "We'll do this. Together."

As they continued their preparations, the weight of their mission pressed heavily on their shoulders. But they knew they were not alone. They had each other, and they had the strength and faith to see their mission through to the end.

16

The Final Stand

The air was thick with anticipation as Dr. Jonathan Reed, Emily Carter, Gabriel Martinez, Anton Graves, and Anya prepared for the inevitable confrontation with The Benefactor. They had come a long way, uncovering ancient secrets and unlocking the relic's power, but they knew the real battle was just beginning.

The safe house was a flurry of activity. Gabriel was setting up additional defenses around the perimeter, while Graves was on the phone, coordinating with his contacts to gather any last-minute intelligence on The Benefactor's movements. Reed and Emily were in the study, pouring over maps and making final adjustments to their plan. Anya, the newly discovered chosen one, was meditating in the living room, focusing her energy and preparing herself for the confrontation ahead.

Reed looked up from the maps, his eyes meeting Emily's. "We've done everything we can to prepare. Now it's up to us to see this through."

Emily nodded, her expression determined. "We've faced incredible odds before, and we've come out stronger each time. We can do this, Jonathan."

Reed smiled, placing a hand on her shoulder. "I know we can. And with Anya by our side, we have a real chance."

As night fell, the team gathered in the living room. The atmosphere was tense but resolute. Reed addressed the group, his voice steady and calm.

"Tonight, we face The Benefactor. We've prepared for this, and we're ready. Anya, you've shown incredible strength and courage. Your connection to the relic is our greatest asset."

Anya nodded, her eyes filled with determination. "I'll do whatever it takes to protect the relic and stop The Benefactor."

Gabriel stepped forward, his expression serious. "We've fortified the safe house as much as we can. If they come, we'll be ready."

Graves added, "I've coordinated with my contacts. We have eyes on The Benefactor's movements. If he makes a move, we'll know about it."

Emily looked around at her team, her heart swelling with pride. "We've come so far, and we've done it together. Whatever happens tonight, we stand as one."

Reed nodded. "Let's do this."

The hours passed slowly, the tension mounting with each passing minute. The team remained vigilant, each member ready to spring into action at a moment's notice. As midnight approached, Gabriel received a call on his secure line. He listened intently, his expression growing grimmer by the second.

"They're coming," Gabriel said, hanging up the phone. "The Benefactor's forces are on their way. We have less than an hour."

Reed took a deep breath, his mind racing. "Everyone, take your positions. We've prepared for this. Let's make it count."

Emily, Gabriel, and Graves moved to their assigned posts, while Anya and Reed stayed in the living room, the relic placed securely in the center of the room. The air was thick with anticipation, the silence only broken by the occasional sound of rustling leaves and distant animal calls.

The first sign of the approaching enemy was a faint rumble in the distance, growing steadily louder. Gabriel, stationed at the perimeter, watched through his night-vision goggles as The Benefactor's forces advanced. He radioed in, his voice calm and focused.

"They're here. Everyone, stay sharp."

Reed glanced at Anya, who was sitting cross-legged on the floor, her eyes closed in deep concentration. "Are you ready?"

Anya opened her eyes, a fierce determination shining in them. "I'm ready. Let's do this."

The first wave of attackers hit the perimeter, triggering a series of traps and alarms. Gabriel and Graves engaged the enemy, their movements swift and precise. The sound of gunfire and shouted commands filled the night, the once peaceful forest now a battleground.

"Emily, cover the east side!" Gabriel shouted, taking down an attacker with a well-placed shot.

Emily responded immediately, her movements fluid and controlled. "I'm on it!"

Reed stayed by Anya's side, his eyes scanning the room for any sign of danger. The relic glowed faintly, its power a comforting presence in the midst of chaos.

Outside, the battle raged on. Gabriel and Graves fought fiercely, using their knowledge of the terrain and their extensive training to hold off the attackers. Emily provided cover fire, her accuracy and speed keeping the enemy at bay.

"We can't let them breach the house!" Gabriel shouted, taking down another attacker. "Hold the line!"

Graves, his expression grim but determined, nodded. "We've got this. Just keep them back."

Inside, Reed and Anya remained focused. Reed could hear the battle outside, the sounds of gunfire and shouting a constant reminder of the danger they faced. He looked at Anya, who was now standing, her hands resting on the relic.

"The Benefactor is coming," she said softly, her eyes closed in concentration. "I can feel his presence."

Reed's heart pounded. "We're ready for him, Anya. Stay focused."

Suddenly, the front door burst open, and The Benefactor stepped inside, flanked by two heavily armed guards. His eyes were cold and calculating, his presence imposing and menacing.

"Dr. Reed," The Benefactor said, his voice smooth and chilling. "We meet at last."

Reed stepped forward, his expression defiant. "This ends here, Benefactor. You won't get the relic."

The Benefactor's lips curled into a cruel smile. "You're brave, Reed. But bravery won't save you."

He raised his hand, and a wave of dark energy surged towards Reed. Anya reacted instantly, raising her own hands and countering with a blast of light from the relic. The two forces clashed in the middle of the room, the energy crackling and sparking.

"You cannot win," The Benefactor hissed, his eyes narrowing. "The relic's power will be mine!"

Reed moved to Anya's side, his voice steady. "We stand together, Anya. Focus on the relic's power."

Anya nodded, her expression fierce. "I won't let him take it."

The battle inside the safe house intensified. The Benefactor's guards moved to attack, but Reed and Anya held them off with the relic's power. Outside, Gabriel, Emily, and Graves continued to fight, their determination unwavering.

As the night wore on, the tide of the battle began to turn. Gabriel and Graves managed to push back the attackers, their combined efforts creating a defensive line that held strong. Emily joined them, her sharpshooting skills proving invaluable.

Inside, Anya and The Benefactor were locked in a fierce struggle, their powers clashing with a force that shook the very foundations of the house. Reed stayed by Anya's side, providing support and encouragement.

"You're stronger than him, Anya," Reed said, his voice filled with conviction. "You can do this."

Anya's eyes blazed with determination. "I can feel the relic's power. It's guiding me."

The Benefactor snarled, his frustration evident. "You cannot defeat me!"

Anya took a deep breath, focusing all her energy on the relic. A blinding light filled the room, emanating from the relic and enveloping The Benefactor. He screamed in rage and pain, his dark energy dissipating in the face of the relic's power.

"No!" The Benefactor cried, his voice filled with desperation. "This cannot be!"

Anya stepped forward, her voice calm and resolute. "It's over, Benefactor. The relic belongs to those who protect and heal, not those who seek to dominate."

With a final, powerful surge of light, The Benefactor was thrown back, his form disintegrating into nothingness. The room fell silent, the air heavy with the aftermath of the battle.

Reed looked at Anya, his heart swelling with pride and relief. "You did it, Anya. You stopped him."

Anya nodded, her expression serene but determined. "We did it, Jonathan. Together."

Outside, the remaining attackers, seeing their leader defeated, began to retreat. Gabriel, Emily, and Graves held their ground, ensuring the safe house was secure.

"We did it," Gabriel said, his voice filled with triumph. "We held them off."

Emily lowered her weapon, her expression one of relief. "It's over. We won."

Graves nodded, his eyes scanning the perimeter. "We need to stay vigilant. There might be stragglers."

As the first light of dawn began to break over the horizon, the team gathered inside the safe house. The battle had been fierce, but they had emerged victorious. The Benefactor was defeated, and the relic was safe.

Reed looked around at his team, his heart filled with gratitude and pride. "We've come a long way, and we've faced incredible challenges. But we did it. Together."

Gabriel nodded, his expression serious but hopeful. "We've proven that we can handle anything that comes our way."

Emily added, "And we'll continue to protect the relic, no matter what."

Graves, his voice steady, said, "We've stopped The Benefactor, but we need to stay vigilant. There will always be those who seek the relic's power."

Anya, her eyes shining with determination, added, "We'll protect the relic and ensure it's used for good. That's our mission."

As the sun rose, casting a golden light over the safe house and the surrounding forest, the team felt a renewed sense of purpose and unity. They had faced their greatest challenge and emerged stronger for it.

Reed stood by the window, looking out at the peaceful landscape. "We've accomplished so much, but our journey is far from over. There will always be new threats, new challenges. But I know we can face them together."

Emily joined him, her hand resting on his shoulder. "We're a team, Jonathan. And as long as we stand together, we can handle anything."

Gabriel, Graves, and Anya gathered around, their expressions filled with determination and hope.

As they stood together, united by their shared purpose and unwavering faith, they knew they were ready to face whatever trials lay ahead. Together, they would protect the relic and ensure its power was used for good.

17

Unveiling Shadows

The aftermath of their victory against The Benefactor was filled with a cautious sense of relief. Dr. Jonathan Reed, Emily Carter, Gabriel Martinez, Anton Graves, and Anya had survived the battle, and the relic was secure. The safe house, though damaged, stood as a testament to their resilience and determination.

Days passed in a blur of repairs and planning. They knew the threat wasn't entirely gone. The Benefactor's defeat had undoubtedly left a power vacuum, and they needed to be ready for whatever came next. The team used the time to regroup and strategize, determined to uncover any lingering threats.

Reed and Emily were in the study, sorting through the remnants of their research. The ancient scrolls and texts were spread out before them, the flickering candlelight casting long shadows on the walls.

"We need to figure out our next steps," Reed said, his voice thoughtful. "The Benefactor may be gone, but his network is still out there."

Emily nodded, her eyes scanning the texts. "Agreed. We should continue our research and see if there are any clues about other potential threats. The relic's power is too great to risk."

Gabriel entered the room, a grim expression on his face. "I've been in contact with my sources. There's been increased activity in some of The

Benefactor's old strongholds. It looks like someone is trying to pick up where he left off."

Reed's eyes narrowed. "We need to find out who's behind this. We can't let them get their hands on the relic."

Graves, who had been standing quietly in the corner, spoke up. "I've been looking into the cult's hierarchy. There are several high-ranking members who could be trying to seize control. We need to identify them and cut off their resources."

Anya, sitting by the window, her hands gently resting on the relic, added, "We need to act quickly. The longer we wait, the more time they have to regroup."

The team decided to split their efforts. Reed and Emily would continue their research, digging into the ancient texts for any clues that might help them understand the relic's power and its connection to the prophecy. Gabriel and Graves would track down the remaining cult members, using their contacts and resources to identify and neutralize any threats. Anya, with her deep connection to the relic, would continue to focus on understanding and harnessing its power.

One afternoon, as Emily and Reed pored over a particularly old and fragile manuscript, Emily found a passage that caught her attention.

"Jonathan, look at this," she said, pointing to the text. "It mentions a ritual—one that could potentially reveal hidden dangers and protect the relic from future threats."

Reed leaned in, his eyes scanning the passage. "This could be exactly what we need. If we can perform this ritual, we might be able to identify any lingering threats and ensure the relic's safety."

Emily nodded. "We should prepare immediately. We don't have time to waste."

That evening, the team gathered in the living room, the air thick with anticipation. The room was dimly lit, the flickering candlelight casting an almost ethereal glow. The relic was placed in the center of the room, surrounded by the symbols and markings necessary for the ritual.

Anya stood at the forefront, her expression calm and focused. "I'll lead the ritual. Everyone else, form a circle around the relic and focus your energy."

They followed her instructions, forming a circle and joining hands. Anya began to chant, her voice steady and clear. The symbols around the relic started to glow, the air humming with energy.

As the ritual progressed, the glow intensified, filling the room with a blinding light. Suddenly, the air seemed to shimmer, and a vision appeared before them—a shadowy figure, cloaked in darkness, standing at the edge of a cliff, looking down at a vast, tumultuous sea.

"This is the threat we face," Anya said, her voice echoing in the room. "A powerful entity, seeking the relic's power. We need to find and stop them."

The vision shifted, showing glimpses of ancient ruins, hidden chambers, and dark rituals. The team watched in awe and trepidation, their minds racing with the implications of what they were seeing.

Reed's voice was firm. "We need to identify these locations. They could hold the key to stopping this new threat."

Gabriel nodded, his expression determined. "I'll start gathering intel. We need to move quickly."

As the vision faded, the room fell silent, the gravity of their mission settling over them. They knew they were facing a formidable enemy, one who would stop at nothing to obtain the relic's power.

The next few days were a blur of activity. Gabriel and Graves worked tirelessly, using their contacts and resources to gather information on the locations shown in the vision. Reed and Emily continued their research, seeking any additional clues that might help them understand the new threat.

One evening, as they gathered around the table, Gabriel shared his findings. "We've identified several of the locations from the vision. One of them is an ancient temple in the heart of the Amazon rainforest. It's said to be a place of great power and significance."

Reed looked thoughtful. "That could be where our new enemy is hiding. We need to get there and stop them before they can harness the relic's power."

Emily nodded. "We should prepare for an expedition. This won't be easy, but it's our best chance."

Anya, her eyes filled with determination, added, "We can do this. Together."

The journey to the Amazon was long and arduous. They traveled by plane, boat, and finally on foot, navigating the dense, humid jungle. The air was thick with the scent of vegetation and the sounds of wildlife, the landscape both beautiful and treacherous.

"We're getting close," Gabriel said, consulting his map. "The temple should be just up ahead."

As they pushed through the dense underbrush, the ancient temple came into view. It was a massive structure, covered in vines and moss, the stone walls etched with intricate carvings and symbols.

"This is it," Reed said, his voice filled with awe. "The place from the vision."

They approached the temple cautiously, their senses heightened. The air was thick with an almost tangible energy, the atmosphere heavy with the weight of centuries of history and power.

Inside, the temple was dimly lit, the walls covered in ancient symbols and markings. They moved carefully, their footsteps echoing in the vast, empty space.

"We need to find the central chamber," Emily said, her voice barely above a whisper. "That's where the ritual will take place."

They navigated the labyrinthine corridors, guided by the symbols on the walls. Finally, they reached a large, circular chamber, the air humming with energy. In the center of the room stood a massive stone altar, covered in ancient carvings.

"This is it," Anya said, her voice filled with reverence. "The place where the ritual will be performed."

Suddenly, a shadowy figure stepped out from the darkness, their eyes gleaming with a malevolent light. "You're too late," the figure hissed. "The ritual has already begun."

Reed stepped forward, his expression defiant. "We won't let you take the relic's power. This ends here."

The figure laughed, a chilling sound that echoed in the chamber. "You cannot stop me. The relic's power will be mine."

Anya moved to the altar, her hands glowing with a soft light. "We'll see about that."

The air crackled with energy as the two forces clashed, the chamber filled with blinding light and the sound of chanting. Anya focused all her energy on the relic, her voice steady and powerful.

"We need to disrupt the ritual!" Emily shouted, her eyes filled with determination.

Gabriel and Graves moved to flank the figure, their movements swift and coordinated. Reed joined Anya at the altar, his hands resting on the relic, adding his energy to hers.

The figure snarled, their eyes blazing with fury. "You will not defeat me!"

Anya's voice rose, her chanting growing more intense. The symbols on the walls began to glow, responding to her words. The air hummed with energy, the power of the relic filling the chamber.

With a final, powerful surge, the light intensified, enveloping the shadowy figure. They screamed in rage and pain, their form disintegrating into nothingness. The chamber fell silent, the air heavy with the aftermath of the battle.

Reed looked at Anya, his heart swelling with pride and relief. "You did it, Anya. You stopped them."

Anya nodded, her expression serene but determined. "We did it, Jonathan. Together."

Gabriel, Emily, and Graves joined them at the altar, their faces filled with a mix of exhaustion and triumph.

"We've stopped the ritual," Gabriel said, his voice filled with relief. "But we need to make sure there are no lingering threats."

Emily nodded. "Agreed. We should continue to monitor the area and make sure the relic is safe."

Graves added, "We've come this far. We can't let our guard down now."

Reed looked around at his team, feeling a renewed sense of purpose and unity. "Then let's make sure the relic is protected. Together, we can handle anything."

As they left the temple, the weight of their mission pressed heavily on their shoulders. They knew the battle was far from over, but they felt a renewed sense of hope and determination. They had faced incredible challenges and emerged victorious, but they knew their journey was far from over.

Back at the safe house, they continued their preparations, strengthening their defenses and planning their next move. They knew they had to stay vigilant, ready to face whatever new threats emerged.

One evening, as they gathered around the table, Reed spoke up. "We've made incredible progress, but we can't let our guard down. There will always be new threats, new challenges. But I know we can face them together."

Emily joined him, her hand resting on his shoulder. "We're a team, Jonathan. And as long as we stand together, we can handle anything."

Gabriel, Graves, and Anya gathered around, their expressions filled with determination and hope.

As they stood together, united by their shared purpose and unwavering faith, they knew they were ready to face whatever trials lay ahead. Together, they would protect the relic and ensure its power was used for good.

18

The Betrayal

The safe house was cloaked in a sense of uneasy calm. Dr. Jonathan Reed, Emily Carter, Gabriel Martinez, Anton Graves, and Anya had faced down formidable threats and emerged victorious, but the specter of future dangers loomed large. They knew their mission to protect the relic was far from over.

Reed sat in the study, the flickering candlelight casting shadows on the walls. He pored over ancient texts, searching for any further insights into the relic's power. Emily entered the room, a look of concern on her face.

"Jonathan, we need to talk," she said, her voice hushed. "I've been thinking about the prophecy and the vision we had in the temple."

Reed looked up, his brow furrowed. "What's on your mind?"

Emily took a seat across from him, her eyes serious. "The vision showed us ancient ruins and dark rituals, but there was something else—a shadowy figure watching us. I can't shake the feeling that we're missing something important."

Reed nodded slowly. "I've been thinking the same thing. There's something about that figure that feels familiar, but I can't quite place it."

Their conversation was interrupted by Gabriel, who entered the study with an urgent expression. "We have a problem. One of my contacts just informed me that there's been a significant uptick in cult activity. They're mobilizing for something big."

Reed's eyes narrowed. "Do we know what their target is?"

Gabriel shook his head. "Not yet, but we need to find out. If they're planning another attack, we have to be ready."

Graves joined them, his expression grim. "I've been doing some digging into the cult's hierarchy. There's a new leader—someone who's been keeping a low profile but has a lot of influence. We need to find out who they are and what they're planning."

Anya entered the room, her presence bringing a sense of calm. "We need to stay focused and vigilant. The relic's power is too great to fall into the wrong hands."

Reed looked around at his team, feeling a mix of determination and unease. "Let's get to work. We need to uncover this new leader and stop whatever they're planning."

The following days were a blur of activity. Gabriel and Graves worked tirelessly, using their contacts and resources to gather intelligence on the cult's movements. Reed and Emily continued their research, seeking any clues that might help them understand the vision and the identity of the shadowy figure. Anya focused on her connection to the relic, meditating and honing her abilities.

One evening, as they gathered around the table, Gabriel shared his findings. "We've identified several key locations where the cult has been active. One of them is an abandoned monastery in the mountains. It's heavily fortified, but it could be their new base of operations."

Reed nodded thoughtfully. "If that's where they're hiding, we need to get in there and find out what they're planning."

Graves added, "We should prepare for the worst. If they've fortified the monastery, they're expecting trouble."

Emily looked at Anya, her eyes filled with determination. "Are you ready for this?"

Anya nodded. "I'm ready. Let's do this."

The journey to the monastery was fraught with tension. They traveled by car, navigating narrow mountain roads and steep inclines. The air grew colder as they ascended, the landscape becoming more rugged and remote.

"We're close," Gabriel said, consulting his map. "The monastery should be just up ahead."

As they approached the monastery, the sense of danger grew. The ancient structure loomed before them, its stone walls covered in ivy and moss. The air was thick with an almost tangible energy, the atmosphere heavy with the weight of centuries of history and power.

Reed and Gabriel scouted the perimeter, noting the guards and security measures. "This place is locked down tight," Gabriel said, his voice low. "We'll need to be careful."

Reed nodded. "Let's move in quietly. We need to find out what they're planning without getting caught."

They slipped through the shadows, moving silently toward the monastery's entrance. The guards were well-trained and alert, but the team's combined skills allowed them to bypass the security undetected.

Inside, the monastery was dimly lit, the air cool and damp. They moved carefully through the corridors, their footsteps echoing in the vast, empty space.

"We need to find the central chamber," Emily whispered. "That's where they'll be conducting the rituals."

As they navigated the labyrinthine corridors, they heard voices coming from a nearby room. Reed signaled for the team to stop, listening intently.

"We need to move quickly," a voice said, filled with urgency. "The ritual must be completed before the next full moon."

Reed's heart pounded. "They're planning something big. We need to find out what it is."

They followed the voices, moving closer to the source. As they approached a large, ornate door, they could hear chanting and the faint hum of energy.

"This is it," Anya whispered. "They're performing a ritual."

Reed nodded. "We need to disrupt it. Emily, Gabriel, and Graves, take out the guards. Anya and I will handle the ritual."

The team moved into action, their movements swift and coordinated. Gabriel and Graves took out the guards with precision, while Emily provided cover. Reed and Anya burst into the chamber, their eyes scanning the scene.

The chamber was filled with cult members, their faces hidden by dark hoods. At the center of the room stood a figure, their presence imposing and menacing.

"You're too late," the figure hissed, their voice echoing in the chamber. "The ritual is almost complete."

Anya stepped forward, her hands glowing with a soft light. "We'll see about that."

The air crackled with energy as the two forces clashed, the chamber filled with blinding light and the sound of chanting. Anya focused all her energy on the relic, her voice steady and powerful.

Reed moved to flank the figure, his eyes locked on their every move. "We won't let you take the relic's power."

The figure laughed, a chilling sound that echoed in the chamber. "You cannot stop me. The relic's power will be mine."

Anya's voice rose, her chanting growing more intense. The symbols on the walls began to glow, responding to her words. The air hummed with energy, the power of the relic filling the chamber.

With a final, powerful surge, the light intensified, enveloping the figure. They screamed in rage and pain, their form disintegrating into nothingness. The chamber fell silent, the air heavy with the aftermath of the battle.

Reed looked at Anya, his heart swelling with pride and relief. "You did it, Anya. You stopped them."

Anya nodded, her expression serene but determined. "We did it, Jonathan. Together."

Gabriel, Emily, and Graves joined them at the altar, their faces filled with a mix of exhaustion and triumph.

"We've stopped the ritual," Gabriel said, his voice filled with relief. "But we need to make sure there are no lingering threats."

Emily nodded. "Agreed. We should continue to monitor the area and make sure the relic is safe."

Graves added, "We've come this far. We can't let our guard down now."

Reed looked around at his team, feeling a renewed sense of purpose and unity. "Then let's make sure the relic is protected. Together, we can handle anything."

As they left the monastery, the weight of their mission pressed heavily on their shoulders. They knew the battle was far from over, but they felt a renewed sense of hope and determination. They had faced incredible challenges and emerged victorious, but they knew their journey was far from over.

Back at the safe house, they continued their preparations, strengthening their defenses and planning their next move. They knew they had to stay vigilant, ready to face whatever new threats emerged.

One evening, as they gathered around the table, Reed spoke up. "We've made incredible progress, but we can't let our guard down. There will always be new threats, new challenges. But I know we can face them together."

Emily joined him, her hand resting on his shoulder. "We're a team, Jonathan. And as long as we stand together, we can handle anything."

Gabriel, Graves, and Anya gathered around, their expressions filled with determination and hope.

"To the future," Gabriel said, raising his hand in a gesture of unity.

"To the relic," Emily added, her voice filled with conviction.

"To protecting what's right," Graves said, his eyes steady.

"And to doing it together," Anya finished, her voice serene and powerful.

As they stood together, united by their shared purpose and unwavering faith, they knew they were ready to face whatever trials lay ahead. Together, they would protect the relic and ensure its power was used for good.

And with that knowledge, they felt a sense of peace and resolve, ready to embrace the future, together.

However, the sense of peace was shattered the next morning. Reed awoke to find the safe house eerily quiet. As he made his way to the living room, he found Anya standing by the window, her expression troubled.

"Anya, what's wrong?" Reed asked, his heart sinking.

Anya turned to face him, her eyes filled with a mixture of sorrow and determination. "Jonathan, I've been having visions. Someone close to us is working against us."

Reed's eyes widened in shock. "What do you mean? Who?"

Before Anya could respond, Gabriel and Graves entered the room, their faces grim. "We need to talk," Gabriel said, his voice tense. "There's been a breach. Someone has been feeding information to the cult."

Reed felt a wave of disbelief wash over him. "Who would do that?"

Graves spoke up, his voice steady. "We don't know yet, but we need to find out. The safety of the relic depends on it."

As they gathered around the table, the atmosphere was charged with tension. They knew they had to uncover the traitor in their midst before it was too late.

"Anya, can your visions help us?" Reed asked, his voice filled with urgency.

Anya nodded. "I believe so. I've seen glimpses, but I need to focus to get a clearer picture."

Emily joined them, her expression determined. "We need to work together. We can't let this betrayal tear us apart."

Gabriel, his eyes filled with resolve, said, "We'll find the traitor and stop them. We've come too far to be undone by this."

Graves added, "We need to stay vigilant and trust each other. We'll get through this, together."

As they began their investigation, the weight of their mission pressed heavily on their shoulders. They knew the battle was far from over, but they felt a renewed sense of hope and determination. They had faced incredible challenges and emerged victorious, but they knew their journey was far from over.

Back at the safe house, they continued their preparations, strengthening their defenses and planning their next move. They knew they had to stay vigilant, ready to face whatever new threats emerged.

One evening, as they gathered around the table, Reed spoke up. "We've made incredible progress, but we can't let our guard down. There will always be new threats, new challenges. But I know we can face them together."

Emily joined him, her hand resting on his shoulder. "We're a team, Jonathan. And as long as we stand together, we can handle anything."

Gabriel, Graves, and Anya gathered around, their expressions filled with determination and hope.

As they stood together, united by their shared purpose and unwavering faith, they knew they were ready to face whatever trials lay ahead. Together, they would protect the relic and ensure its power was used for good.

19

The Final Confrontation

The safe house was buzzing with tension and activity as Dr. Jonathan Reed, Emily Carter, Gabriel Martinez, Anton Graves, and Anya prepared for the final confrontation. The betrayal within their ranks had cast a shadow over their mission, but it had also steeled their resolve. They knew they had to uncover the traitor and stop the cult once and for all.

Reed gathered the team in the living room, the relic placed securely in the center of the table. "We need to find out who the traitor is and stop them before they can do any more damage," he said, his voice firm. "Anya, have you had any more visions?"

Anya nodded, her expression serious. "I've seen glimpses of someone moving in the shadows, feeding information to the cult. It's someone close to us, but the visions are still unclear."

Gabriel leaned forward, his eyes intense. "We need to narrow it down. Who had the opportunity to communicate with the cult?"

Graves spoke up, his voice steady. "We've all had moments alone, but we need to think about who had both the opportunity and the motive."

Emily looked thoughtful. "We've all been under a lot of stress. Someone might have cracked under the pressure."

Reed nodded. "Agreed. But we need to be careful. We can't afford to let suspicion tear us apart."

As they continued their investigation, the tension in the safe house grew. Each member of the team was on edge, wary of each other but determined to uncover the truth. They reviewed security footage, checked communication logs, and scrutinized every detail, but the traitor remained elusive.

One evening, Gabriel approached Reed with a grim expression. "Jonathan, I think I've found something."

Reed's heart pounded. "What is it?"

Gabriel handed him a piece of paper. "I found this hidden in Graves' room. It's a coded message to the cult."

Reed's eyes widened in shock. "Are you sure?"

Gabriel nodded. "I triple-checked it. The evidence is clear."

Reed felt a wave of disbelief wash over him. "We need to confront him. Now."

They gathered in the living room, the atmosphere charged with tension. Graves stood before them, his expression calm but wary.

"Graves," Reed began, his voice steady. "We found a coded message in your room. A message to the cult."

Graves' eyes widened in surprise. "That's impossible. I would never betray you."

Gabriel stepped forward, his eyes hard. "The evidence is clear, Graves. You've been feeding information to the cult."

Graves shook his head, his voice filled with desperation. "I swear, I didn't do it. Someone must have planted that message."

Emily looked at him, her expression conflicted. "Why should we believe you?"

Graves took a deep breath, his eyes filled with sincerity. "Because I've been loyal to this team from the beginning. I would never betray you. You have to believe me."

Anya, her voice calm and steady, said, "We need to be sure. Graves, if you're innocent, help us find the real traitor."

Graves nodded, his expression resolute. "I will. Whatever it takes."

The team continued their investigation, now with Graves' help. They reviewed the evidence again, looking for any inconsistencies or clues they might have missed. As they worked, Anya's visions became clearer, showing more details of the shadowy figure's movements.

One evening, as they gathered around the table, Anya spoke up. "I've seen more of the visions. The traitor is close, but it's not Graves. It's someone who's been hiding in plain sight."

Reed looked at her, his expression filled with hope. "Can you show us?"

Anya nodded, closing her eyes and focusing on the relic. The air around them shimmered, and a vision appeared—a figure moving stealthily through the safe house, planting the coded message in Graves' room. As the vision became clearer, the figure's face was revealed.

Emily gasped. "It's one of Gabriel's contacts. Someone we trusted."

Gabriel's eyes narrowed. "That explains how they got in and out without us noticing. We need to find them and stop them."

Reed's voice was filled with determination. "Let's move. We can't let them get away."

They tracked the traitor to a nearby abandoned warehouse, the tension palpable as they approached the building. Gabriel and Graves moved to flank the entrance, while Reed, Emily, and Anya took position at the front.

"Be ready for anything," Reed whispered, his eyes scanning the area. "We don't know what we're walking into."

They entered the warehouse, moving silently through the dimly lit corridors. The air was thick with dust and the scent of decay, the atmosphere heavy with a sense of foreboding.

As they reached the central chamber, they found the traitor standing before an altar, their hands raised in a dark ritual. The air crackled with energy, the symbols on the walls glowing with an eerie light.

"You're too late," the traitor hissed, their voice filled with malevolence. "The ritual is almost complete. The relic's power will be ours."

Anya stepped forward, her eyes blazing with determination. "We won't let you take the relic."

The traitor laughed, a chilling sound that echoed in the chamber. "You cannot stop us. The cult's power is too great."

Reed moved to flank the traitor, his voice steady. "We'll see about that."

The air crackled with energy as the two forces clashed, the chamber filled with blinding light and the sound of chanting. Anya focused all her energy on the relic, her voice steady and powerful.

"We need to disrupt the ritual!" Emily shouted, her eyes filled with determination.

Gabriel and Graves moved to flank the traitor, their movements swift and coordinated. Reed joined Anya at the altar, his hands resting on the relic, adding his energy to hers.

The traitor snarled, their eyes blazing with fury. "You will not defeat us!"

Anya's voice rose, her chanting growing more intense. The symbols on the walls began to glow, responding to her words. The air hummed with energy, the power of the relic filling the chamber.

With a final, powerful surge, the light intensified, enveloping the traitor. They screamed in rage and pain, their form disintegrating into nothingness. The chamber fell silent, the air heavy with the aftermath of the battle.

Reed looked at Anya, his heart swelling with pride and relief. "You did it, Anya. You stopped them."

Anya nodded, her expression serene but determined. "We did it, Jonathan. Together."

Gabriel, Emily, and Graves joined them at the altar, their faces filled with a mix of exhaustion and triumph.

"We've stopped the ritual," Gabriel said, his voice filled with relief. "But we need to make sure there are no lingering threats."

Emily nodded. "Agreed. We should continue to monitor the area and make sure the relic is safe."

Graves added, "We've come this far. We can't let our guard down now."

Reed looked around at his team, feeling a renewed sense of purpose and unity. "Then let's make sure the relic is protected. Together, we can handle anything."

As they left the warehouse, the weight of their mission pressed heavily on their shoulders. They knew the battle was far from over, but they felt a renewed sense of hope and determination. They had faced incredible challenges and emerged victorious, but they knew their journey was far from over.

Back at the safe house, they continued their preparations, strengthening their defenses and planning their next move. They knew they had to stay vigilant, ready to face whatever new threats emerged.

One evening, as they gathered around the table, Reed spoke up. "We've made incredible progress, but we can't let our guard down. There will always be new threats, new challenges. But I know we can face them together."

Emily joined him, her hand resting on his shoulder. "We're a team, Jonathan. And as long as we stand together, we can handle anything."

Gabriel, Graves, and Anya gathered around, their expressions filled with determination and hope.

As they stood together, united by their shared purpose and unwavering faith, they knew they were ready to face whatever trials lay ahead. Together, they would protect the relic and ensure its power was used for good.

20

The Resolution

The safe house was finally quiet. After the intense confrontation with the traitor and the relentless pursuit of the cult, the team felt a momentary peace. Dr. Jonathan Reed, Emily Carter, Gabriel Martinez, Anton Graves, and Anya had faced the darkest of threats and emerged victorious. But their mission wasn't over. They had to ensure that the relic was protected for good.

As the first light of dawn broke over the horizon, Reed stood by the window, looking out at the tranquil landscape. Emily joined him, her presence a comforting reminder of their shared journey.

"We've come so far," Reed said softly, his voice filled with a mix of awe and exhaustion. "But I can't shake the feeling that there's more to do."

Emily nodded, her expression thoughtful. "The relic's power is immense. We've managed to protect it, but we need to ensure it remains safe. Permanently."

Reed turned to face her, a determined look in his eyes. "Agreed. We need to find a way to shield the relic from anyone who might seek to misuse it."

The team gathered in the living room, the relic resting on the table between them. The atmosphere was one of quiet determination and lingering tension. They knew their journey was nearing its end, but they had to be vigilant until the very last moment.

Gabriel broke the silence, his voice steady. "We need a permanent solution. Something that will ensure the relic's power is protected, no matter what."

Graves nodded, his expression serious. "I've been thinking about that. What if we could conceal the relic in a place where no one could find it? Somewhere only we know about."

Anya, her eyes focused on the relic, spoke up. "There's a way. The ancient texts mentioned a ritual that could bind the relic's power to a sacred place, effectively hiding it from those with ill intentions."

Reed's eyes widened. "Do you think we can perform the ritual?"

Anya nodded. "I believe so. But we need to find the right place—a place of great spiritual significance."

Emily's eyes lit up with realization. "The temple in the Amazon. It's a place of immense power and sacredness. It could be the perfect location."

Gabriel looked thoughtful. "It's risky, but it's our best shot. We need to move quickly before anyone else finds out what we're planning."

Reed stood, his expression resolute. "Then let's prepare. This will be our final mission."

The journey to the Amazon was both familiar and daunting. They retraced their steps through dense jungles and treacherous terrain, their determination unwavering. The temple loomed ahead, its ancient walls and towering spires a testament to centuries of history and power.

As they entered the temple, the air was thick with anticipation. The symbols on the walls seemed to glow faintly, as if acknowledging their presence. Anya led the way, her connection to the relic guiding her.

"We need to find the central chamber," Anya said, her voice filled with a sense of purpose. "That's where the ritual must take place."

They navigated the labyrinthine corridors, the atmosphere heavy with an almost tangible energy. Finally, they reached the central chamber, a vast, circular room with a massive stone altar at its center.

"This is it," Reed said, his voice echoing in the chamber. "Let's get started."

They set up the altar, placing the relic in the center. Anya began to chant, her voice steady and powerful, filling the chamber with an ancient melody. The symbols on the walls began to glow brighter, responding to her words.

Emily and Reed joined hands, their voices rising in harmony with Anya's. Gabriel and Graves stood guard, their eyes scanning the chamber for any signs of danger.

The air around them shimmered with energy, the power of the relic filling the space. Anya's chanting grew more intense, her connection to the relic deepening with each word.

"We're doing it," Anya said, her voice filled with awe. "The ritual is working."

The light from the symbols intensified, enveloping the relic in a radiant glow. The air hummed with a powerful energy, the very walls of the temple seeming to vibrate with the force of the ritual.

Suddenly, the chamber shook, and a deep, resonant voice filled the air. "Who dares to bind the power of the relic?"

Reed's heart pounded. "We are the protectors of the relic. We seek to bind its power to this sacred place, to keep it safe from those who would misuse it."

The voice echoed through the chamber, filled with a mix of curiosity and authority. "You seek to protect the relic? Prove your worthiness."

Anya stepped forward, her eyes blazing with determination. "We have faced countless trials and emerged victorious. We have fought to protect the relic and its power. We are worthy."

The air around them crackled with energy, and a figure appeared before them—a tall, ethereal being, radiating power and wisdom. "You have shown great courage and determination. The relic shall be bound to this place, protected for all time."

The figure raised its hands, and the light around the relic intensified, enveloping it in a blinding glow. The air hummed with energy, the power of the relic merging with the sacredness of the temple.

When the light faded, the relic was gone, its power now bound to the temple. The chamber was filled with a sense of peace and fulfillment, the weight of their mission lifted from their shoulders.

Reed looked at Anya, his eyes filled with gratitude. "You did it, Anya. We did it."

Anya nodded, her expression serene. "The relic is safe. Its power is protected."

Gabriel and Graves joined them, their faces filled with relief and triumph. "We've done it," Gabriel said, his voice filled with pride. "The relic is finally safe."

Emily smiled, her eyes shining with happiness. "We can finally rest, knowing we've fulfilled our mission."

As they left the temple, the sense of accomplishment and peace was almost overwhelming. They had faced incredible challenges and emerged victorious, their bond stronger than ever. The relic was safe, its power protected for all time.

Back at the safe house, they gathered one last time, the atmosphere filled with a sense of closure and unity. Reed looked around at his team, his heart swelling with pride and gratitude.

"We've done it," Reed said, his voice filled with emotion. "We've protected the relic and ensured its power is used for good. We've fulfilled our mission."

Emily joined him, her hand resting on his shoulder. "We're a team, Jonathan. And as long as we stand together, we can handle anything."

Gabriel, Graves, and Anya gathered around, their expressions filled with determination and hope.

"To the future," Gabriel said, raising his hand in a gesture of unity.

"To the relic," Emily added, her voice filled with conviction.

"To protecting what's right," Graves said, his eyes steady.

"And to doing it together," Anya finished, her voice serene and powerful.

As they stood together, united by their shared purpose and unwavering faith, they knew they were ready to face whatever trials lay ahead. Together, they had protected the relic and ensured its power was used for good.

And with that knowledge, they felt a sense of peace and resolve, ready to embrace the future, together.

The sun rose over the horizon, casting a golden light over the safe house and the surrounding landscape. The team stood together, their hearts filled with hope and determination. They had faced their greatest challenge and emerged stronger for it, their bond unbreakable.

Reed looked at his team, his voice filled with pride. "We've come a long way, and we've faced incredible challenges. But we did it. Together."

Emily nodded, her eyes shining with happiness. "We're a team, Jonathan. And as long as we stand together, we can handle anything."

Gabriel, Graves, and Anya joined them, their expressions filled with determination and hope.

As they stood together, united by their shared purpose and unwavering faith, they knew they were ready to face whatever trials lay ahead. Together, they had protected the relic and ensured its power was used for good.

About the author

Rene' brings a uniquely contemplative voice to her writing, shaped by a life rich in diverse experiences. Born and raised amid the historic streets of Washington, D.C., she absorbed the capital's vibrant culture before spending her formative teenage years in Maryland, where she experienced the dynamic contrast of urban and suburban life.

Known in her youth for her quiet observance, Rene' developed an early appreciation for the power of listening and learning from others. She found particular connection with older generations, whose stories and wisdom would later influence her storytelling. This natural inclination toward intergenerational dialogue fostered a deep understanding of human experience across different eras, a theme that resonates throughout her work.

A defining chapter in Rene' 's life came with her service in the U.S. Army during Desert Storm. Her military experience not only instilled discipline and resilience but also provided profound insights into human nature and teamwork - elements that now form the backbone of her narrative style. As a veteran-turned-author, she brings an authentic perspective to her storytelling, infusing her work with both sensitivity and strength.

Through her writing, Rene' aims to illuminate the positive aspects of life's journey, drawing from her varied experiences to create stories that resonate with readers of all backgrounds.

Readers can discover more about Renée's work at www.books-by-rene.store